"I believe the feeling is mutual."

She looked at Cadell then, daring to meet his gaze directly without sliding quickly away. His gaze was warm, inviting, suggesting delights she could barely imagine. Yet he remained a perfect gentleman with her. He was getting past her guard, little by little.

An electric shock seemed to zing between them. Something invisible was trying to push her closer to him.

But then he broke their gaze and turned. "Wanna come inside and rummage through my fridge before I take you back?" He glanced at his watch. "I go on duty in a couple of hours."

Yup, in addition to sexual attraction, she was learning to like him a whole lot. Sexual attraction she could deal with. She'd sent away more than one guy over the years because she wasn't going to get that close to anyone.

But liking? That could be even more of a risk.

CORNERED IN CONARD COUNTY

New York Times Bestselling Author

RACHEL LEE

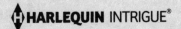

Recycling programs
for this product may
not exist in your area.

ISBN-13: 978-0-373-75692-6

Cornered in Conard County

Copyright © 2017 by Susan Civil Brown

HARLEQUIN®
www.Harlequin.com

Printed in U.S.A.

Rachel Lee was hooked on writing by the age of twelve and practiced her craft as she moved from place to place all over the United States. This *New York Times* bestselling author now resides in Florida and has the joy of writing full-time.

Books by Rachel Lee

Harlequin Intrigue

Conard County: The Next Generation

Cornered in Conard County

Harlequin Romantic Suspense

Conard County: The Next Generation

Undercover in Conard County
Conard County Marine
A Conard County Spy
A Secret in Conard County
Conard County Witness
Playing with Fire
Undercover Hunter
Snowstorm Confessions
Deadly Hunter
Killer's Prey
Rocky Mountain Lawman
What She Saw
Rancher's Deadly Risk
The Widow's Protector
Guardian in Disguise

Visit the Author Profile page at Harlequin.com for more titles.

CAST OF CHARACTERS

Dory Lake—A computer graphics designer fleeing from a murderous brother just freed from prison.

Cadell Marcus—A deputy sheriff and K-9 trainer for Conard County who gives Dory a guard dog.

Betty Casell—An old friend of Dory's who offers her a place to stay.

George Lake—Dory's brother, who killed their parents when she was seven and now wants to kill her.

Flash and Dasher—Two highly trained K-9s.

Prologue

Dory stirred from sleep and tried to cover her ears. Daddy was fighting with her big brother, George, again. But later she realized it sounded different. Voices shouted, but was Mommy laughing? It didn't sound like Mommy's fun laugh.

Curious, Dory climbed out of bed, picked up her favorite bunny and stood at the head of the stairs. Daddy was still shouting. Sticking her thumb in her mouth, she stared at the pool of light pouring out of the kitchen downstairs. Mommy made a strange sound, and curiosity pushed Dory to descend.

Before she was halfway down, things got very quiet and she stopped. She wondered if she'd get into trouble for being out of bed. Daddy and Mommy were very strict about that. Once in bed, stay in bed until morning. George laughed about it, but he said Mommy and Daddy needed grown-up time. But George was mostly grown-up and he got to go out at night. That was probably why they were yelling. Dory hesitated. The yelling was gone.

But then she heard a strange sound and came downstairs the rest of the way. Bunny tucked under her arm, thumb in her mouth, she turned toward the light spilling from the kitchen.

Everything was red. Like paint. It was everywhere and Mommy and Daddy were on the floor covered in the paint. George stood there, his face all tight and funny as he looked at her.

"It's okay, Dory. I made the bad man run away." He squatted and held out his arms to her.

Usually Dory ran straight toward him, but George was covered with the red paint, too, and she didn't like that.

"Dory? Come here, pumpkin."

She saw what was in his hand. A knife. It was all red, too. Why was everything so red?

Some instinct pierced her, and terror shook her out of her confusion. She didn't know what was going on, but she ceased to think. Something deep within her reacted, and she ran out the front door onto the street and started screaming...screaming...screaming.

Chapter One

Screaming.

Dory Lake awoke with her own screams ringing in her ears. The minute her eyes popped open, blessed lamplight greeted her, and for a moment, just a moment, she felt safe.

She remembered what she had seen, but over twenty-five years the nightmares had grown less frequent. Now they were coming back again, every night or several times a night.

Because her brother was about to be released from prison.

She sat up quickly, and was relieved when she didn't grow light-headed. She had low blood pressure, and sometimes it took her by surprise, causing her to faint briefly. A minor thing, a mere nuisance most of the time.

Drenched with sweat, she climbed from bed and walked into the small bathroom to shower. He wasn't out yet. Not yet. She was okay.

But the dream had brought that terrifying night back. All the intervening years hadn't expunged the memory, although it had been troubling her less and less. But ever since she had learned George was about to complete his sentence, the nightmares had returned. Every single night. No escape.

There was no reason to think George would have any interest in her when she'd never spoken about any of it, and he couldn't be convicted of the murder again anyway, she told herself repeatedly as the cold water pounded her. As she'd been telling herself ever since she got the news. He couldn't even be interested in her inheritance which was locked up in an unbreakable trust, a trust his lawyer had told him about.

Hell, he probably wouldn't even be able to find her. The last name Lake was an extremely common one.

At last she toweled off, climbed into a fresh night-gown and robe, and started downstairs. No more sleep tonight. Too bad, she was moving into her own place tomorrow…or was it today?

Downstairs the kitchen light was on. Her friend Betty made sure the house stayed reasonably well lit at night. For Dory, who couldn't stand waking in the dark.

But when she stepped into the gaily colored kitchen, she found Betty was already there with a fresh pot of coffee. Betty sat at the table, mugs, spoons and sugar at the ready, along with a plate of cookies. Her short graying hair looked tousled and, true to her taste, she wore a zip-up robe that was nearly psychedelic with cat faces. Betty was determined to become the cat lady. So far she'd acquired only three, all of whom were now swirling, wondering if it was time for breakfast.

"I heard the shower," Betty said. "Again?"

"Again. I'm sorry I woke you."

"What kind of friend would I be if I got annoyed by that? I don't have nightmares like yours, but I've had them. Nice to have someone near when they wake you." Betty bit her lower lip. "Are you *sure* you should move out? I can't stand thinking of you all alone."

Dory slid into one of the chairs. "I've been living on my own since college. I can't let George's release take my independence from me. Anyway, there's absolutely no reason he should want to find me. He served his time and I'm no threat. After all this time, we're strangers. And, as you know, I need to get back to my job."

Of course, those brave words ignored the fact that she'd run all the way to Conard County, Wyoming, from Kansas at Betty's invitation, when she'd learned her brother would soon be released and the nightmares had returned. Packed up and fled, if she was honest about it. Saying George wouldn't want to find her felt like whistling past the graveyard.

Betty, even back in the days when she taught Dory's high school English class, had been blunt, not one to pull her punches. So it bothered Dory that Betty had felt she should come here.

Apparently Betty didn't quite believe George wouldn't come looking for Dory. Or maybe she had just believed the move would ease Dory's nightmares. So much for that.

The coffee went down well, as did a cookie, and soon her fears eased enough that one of the cats, a ginger tabby called simply Ginger, was willing to leap on her lap and beg for pets.

Such a soothing scene, Dory thought as she rubbed the ginger cat's cheeks and elicited a surprisingly loud purr. Her relaxation deepened, and she thought that maybe she'd better get a cat herself.

"So therapy's out?" Betty asked quietly.

"I've been through years of it. I doubt they can do any more."

"Maybe not, but you're older now." Then Betty hesitated. "I have a friend I want you to meet this morning."

Dory stiffened a bit. She'd been here a week, and so far she'd avoided getting drawn into a social circle. She didn't know if she was ready for that, and anyway, she'd never been good at it.

"Oh, relax," Betty said, reading her reaction correctly. "Someday you'll want out of that shell, but I doubt it's going to be right away. You've been in it for too many years. No, this is a special kind of friend. He's the K-9 officer for the sheriff. He trains the dogs and other officers. Anyway, I want you to meet him."

"Why?"

"Well, apart from the fact that he's got two nasty ostriches he never wanted and can't get rid of, which I find hysterically funny and interesting, he has lots of dogs. I think you need a dog to keep you company."

Dory stared at her. "Why? I was thinking about a cat."

Betty smiled. "Think about it, Dory. What's going to make you feel safer? A guard dog or a guard cat?"

Almost in spite of herself, Dory laughed. "You make a point."

"I always have," Betty said.

Back in those long-ago days when Betty had been her sophomore English teacher, Betty alone had showed the infinite patience Dory needed to let someone become close to her. Betty's campaign had lasted well beyond high school until, finally, surprise of surprises, Dory realized she had a true friend.

No one else had come so close to her.

"Oh, and you're not moving today," Betty said, reaching for a cookie.

Dory preferred deciding things for herself. "Why?" she asked, a bit sharply.

Betty ignored her tone. "Because there was a voice mail message this morning. It'll be two more days before your high-speed internet is wired in. You need that to work, don't you?"

"They promised to do it today," she answered, but realized getting upset about it wouldn't help anything. Since she got here, Betty had offered to take her out to the community college to use the internet there. At home, Betty had little need for a high-speed connection. But her connection was good enough to pick up email, so Dory hadn't taken Betty up on her offer to go to the college. Anyway, the college didn't have what she needed.

But she couldn't stop working indefinitely and it had been too long already. Email sufficed for a short time only. "I need my connection," she said presently. "Two more days, huh?"

"What exactly do you do that keeps you online most of the day?" Betty asked. "I get the souped-up computer with all the whiz-bang gizmos, multiple monitors, a graphics card that would break anyone's bank account…but you can get your email here, right?"

Dory smiled faintly and poured herself a little more coffee. "I don't do graphic art all by myself. I work with a team most of the time. Being able to chat back and forth and share files is essential."

"I see." Betty furrowed her brow. "Well, I can call the company again and see if they can hop to it. I know Wil Gladston, and he should be able to pull a string or two."

Dory reached out to touch Betty's arm. "A couple of days more won't make or break my situation. Everyone knew I'd be off grid for a while. And everyone knows I'm moving. At least we're not under a tight deadline pressure right now."

"If you're sure," Betty said. "Things happen so differently in a small town, you know. Nobody's in a rush without a reason. I'm sure if I explained about your job…"

Dory shook her head. "It's all right," she insisted. "I've got more than enough to keep me busy, and I can check email on your connection, as you said."

She decided it was time to change the subject. She didn't want Betty worrying about her. "So this guy with the dogs? You said he has ostriches? Really?"

Betty's face smoothed, and a grin was born. "Two of 'em. Nasty critters."

"Then why does he have them?"

"He doesn't know." Betty laughed. "It's such a funny

story. Cadell's dad died unexpectedly. When Cadell came home for the funeral, he found he'd not only inherited the ranch, but those damn ostriches, as well. No clue why or how they got there." She leaned forward a bit, still grinning. "Now I gotta tell you, that man is patient beyond belief and seldom cusses. But those birds can wind him up enough to cuss a blue streak. A very inventive blue streak. A show well worth watching."

Dory was smiling herself, verging on a laugh. "Why doesn't he get rid of them?"

"You think he hasn't tried? Oh, my." Betty threw her head back and laughed. "I'll let him tell you. It's a story and a half."

Several hours later as she dressed to go meet this K-9 guy with Betty, Dory wondered why she should need protection. Her brother always had been good to Dory before that night. More tolerant than most brothers that age with a girl of seven. Their relationship had been warm and loving.

Until that night. Every time she remembered him standing there drenched in blood, holding out his hand, holding a bloody knife, she wondered what his intentions had been. Would he have killed her, too? She still didn't understand why he'd killed her parents. Or how it was he hadn't gotten a life sentence.

But all those unanswered questions ate at her, and the nightmares proved that she was afraid of him to this day. Maybe that fear was groundless, but he *had* killed their parents and offered no good explanation for any of it that she had ever heard, not even much later when she was old enough to ask the questions.

Impatient with herself, she yanked on a polo shirt to go with her jeans and tried to look forward to seeing the nasty ostriches. And the dogs. She'd always liked dogs.

Just one step at a time, one day at a time, until her emotional upset settled once again. She'd be fine.

CADELL MARCUS STOOD near the ostrich pen, eyeing his pair of nemeses with restrained dislike. Except for some pretty feathers, these were the ugliest-looking birds he'd ever seen. He was a tall man, but they towered over him, a fact they never seemed to let him forget. Dinosaurs. Why weren't they extinct?

But there they stood, edged into the small pen he sometimes needed to use because, occasionally, despite ostrich demands, he needed his corral for things besides them.

Nor did he ever let himself forget those birds could kick him to death with a few blows. Not that they tried, but they'd sure given him the evil eye often enough, and when they stopped being scared of him and quit hunkering down, they had discovered great delight in pecking at his cowboy hats. Two expensive ones had bitten the dust before he'd realized what he really needed was a football helmet when he came within six feet.

He'd rounded them up into the small pen today, because Betty Cassell was bringing that friend of hers out to see about a guard dog. Betty had given him only the sketchiest of accounts as to why she felt it necessary, so he hoped he'd get more of the story when they arrived.

In the meantime...those damn ostriches would have to behave whether they liked it or not. At least the electrified fencing contained them. He couldn't imagine trying to catch them if they ever got out. He'd need Mike Windwalker, the veterinarian, with his magic dart gun.

They were glaring at him now. He glared back. "You two don't know how lucky you are that I don't send you to a boot factory."

He finally heard a motor approaching and the sound of tires on the gravel. Both birds redirected their attention and backed up, settling low to the ground in a protective posture. "Stay that way," he suggested, then went to greet his guests.

A smile lit his face the instant he saw Betty. Something about her always made him smile. But the woman who climbed out the other side of the car made him catch his breath. He wouldn't have thought a living woman could have the face of a Botticelli angel, complete with long blond hair, but this one did. She caught and held his gaze until he realized he was being rude.

Then he saw the rest of her. Oh, man, no angel could have a body like that. Or at least shouldn't, because it caused an immediate firestorm in him, jeans and loose blue polo shirt notwithstanding.

"Hey, Cadell," Betty called with a wave.

Cadell gathered himself with effort, mentally

whipped himself back into line and focused on her. He approached with outstretched hand. "Good to see you, Betty."

"Same here," she said, shaking his hand. "And this is my friend Dory Lake."

He turned and could no longer avoid looking at her. Simply breathtaking. With blue eyes the color of a summer sky. At one glance she made him feel dusty, unkempt and out of his league.

But she smiled warmly and extended her hand. When he reached for it, the touch was electric. "I heard about your ostriches."

"Not everything, I'm sure." Well, at least he could still talk, and the ostriches provided a bridge over his reaction to her. Never had a woman left him feeling so…well, hell, he was a cop. No one, male or female, ever left him gobsmacked.

Until now.

"Betty said you inherited the birds with the ranch?"

His grin returned. "Yup. I have no idea where they came from, just that apparently my dad had been taking care of them. Long enough to put in electrified fencing so they can't escape. So there they are." He turned and pointed to the pen. "Don't get too close— they peck."

She smiled, a beautiful expression. "Betty says you want to get rid of them?"

"To a good home somewhere the climate will suit them better. So far, no takers."

"I have to confess I had no idea how big they are," Dory said.

"Eight feet or so at maturity. Say, let's go look at the dogs. They make much better company."

He could feel the evil eyes following him as he led the ladies around his two-story ranch house to the dog run and kennels out back. At the moment he had six in various stages of training, mostly Belgian Malinois, but a German shepherd had joined the mix. In all he had ten kennels with access to fenced areas behind. It would have been unkind to expect them to live on concrete with their messes.

The dogs stood immediately, curious, ears pricked attentively. No barking, no crazy antics. Training showed.

He waited while the ladies looked them over, then Dory surprised him, pointing at the shepherd. "That's a different breed."

"Most people don't even notice," he answered. "Yeah, he's a German shepherd. The others are Belgian Malinois, sometimes called Belgian shepherds."

She looked at him with those blue eyes. "Do they behave differently?"

"A bit. The Malinois can be stubborn. He needs a good handler, but he's also more powerful than he looks. A great police dog. But the shepherd is more obedient, so…" He shrugged. "I've worked with both breeds over the last decade or so, and I love them both. Either breed would make you a good guard dog, but they're energetic. I hope you like to jog."

Her smiled dawned, and he felt his heart skip. Too much perfection?

"As it happens, I jog every day. Two or three miles. Would that be enough?"

"Like anything else, the faster you go, the faster they tire. They've got a lot of endurance, though, which is why they're such good working dogs. Both are also courageous to a fault."

He watched her look from dog to dog almost pensively. He pointed to two on the right end of the kennels. "Those two are almost ready to join the force as K-9s. Their handlers are about to finish training with them. But the other four are at various points in training, and any would make a good guard dog quite quickly."

She nodded. "Which would you recommend for a computer geek who can forget the time of day half the time?"

Cadell couldn't suppress a laugh. "The shepherd would lie at your feet and give you soulful looks. The Malinois might poke you with his nose to get your attention. But…they can all be mischievous. No guarantees on that."

He didn't expect her to decide just by looking, so he opened two of the kennels, freeing the shepherd and one Malinois. Far from racing away along the dog run, they stepped out, surveyed the newcomers, then politely sniffed both Betty and Dory. Once their immediate curiosity was satisfied, both sat on their haunches and waited expectantly.

"I've never seen dogs so well trained," Dory exclaimed.

"Most people don't want to be jumped on," Cadell replied. "They will if you want them to, but I don't recommend it. Hold out your hand palm up. Once they've sniffed it, you should be able to pet them."

DORY LOVED THE look of both dogs. Something about their eyes, at once alert and…empathetic? Did dogs feel empathy? She had no idea, but she was drawn to squat down so they were at eye level. Both dogs met her gaze steadily, which surprised her. She held out both hands, one to each dog, and as promised got nosed. Only then did she reach out to bury her fingers in their thick coats.

She'd never had a pet, she knew next to nothing about what she was getting into, but she knew in that instant that she very much wanted one of these dogs. She had the worst urge to wrap her arms around both their necks and hug them.

Amazed by her own response, one she almost never felt with people, she sat back on her heels and tried to regain her composure. "They're both beautiful. I have to decide right now?"

"Of course not," Cadell answered. "But it might help if we went out in the paddock and played a bit with them. They have different personalities, just like people do. One of them will catch your eye more than the other."

So, for a little while, Dory forgot everything else as they played fetch with tennis balls and tug with a twisted rope. In the end she settled on the Malinois. Yeah, she could see the mischief in him, but she loved his coloration, a dark muzzle and legs that looked like they were cased in dark socks. There was something else, too, something that happened when their eyes met. It was almost as if the dog were saying, "I'm yours."

Crazy, she thought, but she announced her decision. A Malinois it would be. As she turned toward Cadell to tell him, a smile on her lips, she saw the heat in his gaze. Quickly shuttered, but not so quickly she didn't feel a responsive heat in herself.

She swiftly looked to the dog that had stapled itself to the side of her leg. Cadell Marcus was a very attractive man. Well built, a strong face and a great smile. He stood there in his sweatshirt, hands on narrow jean-clad hips, waiting, and she didn't dare look at him again.

These kinds of feelings frightened her almost as much as her nightmares. She was broken, she thought as she stroked the dog's head. Broken in so many ways, and all those ways led back to George. A spark of anger stiffened her spine.

"This one," she said to Cadell.

He smiled. "You're already a pair. He really likes

you. Great choice. We can start training you right now, if you like."

"Training me?" she asked, surprised.

"Training you," he repeated. "All we're going to do is ask him to use his native personality and skills for your benefit. But you need to know how to bring that out of him."

Looking down at the dog, she felt a real eagerness to get started, to develop a relationship with him. "Sure. What's his name?"

"Flash. But you can call him something else if you want."

She smiled again. "Flash is a good name, especially since I'm a geek."

He laughed and turned toward Betty. "It'll be a couple of hours. If you want to stay, there's coffee and snacks in the kitchen."

Betty glanced at her watch. "I'll be back about twelve thirty, okay? You two have fun."

Cadell waved and returned his attention to Dory, leaving her inexplicably breathless. "Let's go," he said.

NEARLY A THOUSAND miles away in a Missouri state prison, George Lake sat in the yard enjoying the taste of sun. Two more days and he'd be out of here. He had to school himself to patience.

At least no one bothered him anymore. He'd grown strong and tough here, and he intended to take both away with him. He would also take distrust. He knew better than to tell even his friends here what he had in mind. Any one of them could blab, and this time no one was going to be able to link him to what he had planned.

So he sat there smiling, turning his face up to the welcome sun. Life was about to become so good. Just one little hitch ahead of him.

"Say, man," said a familiar voice. Ed Krank sat beside him.

"Hey," George answered, opening his eyes just briefly to assess the yard for building trouble. There were no warnings.

"So whatcha gonna do? Man, I can't believe you're getting out in two days. How can you stand waiting?"

"I've been waiting for twenty-five years. Two days look short." Which was a lie. Right now they looked endlessly long.

"They don't give you much when you leave here," Ed remarked. "You got something lined up?"

"Sure do."

"Good for you. Somebody said you had some money."

George managed not to stiffen. He knew where that came from. Even the oldest news got passed around here relentlessly, because there was so little new to talk about. Money had been mentioned in the papers long ago. "Anything I inherited they took away from me when I was convicted. No, man, nothing like that."

"Too bad."

Except that he'd been using the computers at the prison library when he could and had been tracking his little sister's life. She still had most of the life insurance, because she'd gotten money for the house, too. And she apparently had a tidy little business going.

If something happened to her, say, something deadly, he'd be her only heir. This time he'd get it, because this time he was determined that they weren't going to link him to any of it.

Oh, he'd learned a lot of lessons here, just listening, occasionally acting.

Dory might have disappeared a couple of weeks ago, but he'd find her. She had to surface online again, and he'd spent some time in classes learning how to use those skills, as well.

He'd find her. Then he just had to make it look like an accident.

"I'll be fine," he told Ed, not that he cared what Ed thought about it one way or another. "I made some plans."

Ed laughed. "Got plenty of time in here to make plans."

"No kidding," George answered, smiling. "There's work waiting for me." He just wasn't going to say what kind.

"Good for you," Ed said approvingly. "I'm getting out in eight months. Maybe you can set up a job for me."

"I'll see what I can do." But he had no intention of that. Remove Dory, get his inheritance and then get the hell out of this country.

Closing his eyes, he imagined himself sitting on

a beach, with plenty of beautiful women wandering around.

Oh, yeah. Not much longer.

But between here and there lay Dory. Such a shame, he thought. If she'd just stayed in bed like she was supposed to, he could have slipped away and covered his tracks. Neither of them would have had to endure this hell.

But she had disobeyed a strict rule, had come down those stairs and walked in on him. She wouldn't even listen when he tried to tell her he'd gotten rid of the bad man.

Instead she had run screaming into the streets, and soon the night had been filled with lights spilling from houses, people running to help her, and cop cars. He'd tried to run, but it was too late to cover his tracks. She was to blame for that. Her and no one else.

So, she'd get what was coming to her. He'd paid for his crimes, and now he deserved the life he should have had all along. Instead she owned it all.

Well, he was just going to have to change that. Given the group she worked for, it wouldn't be long before he located her.

Then he'd have to figure out how to cause her a fatal accident.

He almost felt a twinge for the little girl she used to be, but the intervening years had hardened any softness that might have been left in him, and she was no longer a little girl who sat on his lap for a bedtime story.

No, she was grown now, and not once had she written or tried to visit him.

It was all over between them. Well, except for ending her existence the way he'd ended their parents'. Only much more cleanly, making sure it didn't look like murder.

His smile widened a bit. He'd bet she thought he'd forgotten all about her. Stupid woman. She'd cost him everything.

Chapter Two

Two hours later, Dory sat in the middle of the dog run, laughing while Flash licked her face. "He doesn't wear out!"

"Not easily," Cadell agreed. "I guess he's chosen you, too. He needs a little more training with you to cement his role, but if you want you can take him back to Betty's with you."

"She has three cats!"

"They might not like it, but Flash will leave them alone. Okay, I'll keep him here for now. I wouldn't mind tightening up his training some more." He dropped down onto the ground beside her, knees up slightly, arms hanging loosely over them. "Betty told me a bit about what's going on. Want to talk a little?"

She tensed. Here she'd been having such a good time, and now this popped up. She wanted to resent him for it but could understand his curiosity. After all, he was training a guard dog for her. "Will it help?"

He caught her gaze and held it, an electric moment that conveyed compassion, as well. "Up to you, but I usually like to know what kind of threats my dogs will be working on. It allows me to hone their training. A bomb-sniffing dog doesn't always make a good attack dog."

She nodded slowly, looking down at her crossed legs and Flash's head, now settled comfortably on her lap. Her fingers were buried in his scruff, the massaging movement comforting him as well as her. Dang dog was magical, she thought.

Finally she sighed. "Betty probably told you the important parts. My older brother killed our parents. I was seven and I walked in on it. Anyway, somehow he only got twenty-five years, not life, and he's getting out soon."

She turned to look at him again, her voice becoming earnest. "I have no reason to think he'll be the least interested in finding me. I haven't seen or talked to him since that night. He never even wrote me from prison. But… I'm having a lot of nightmares at night, and no matter how much I tell myself…"

"You still can't quite believe he's not a threat to you," he completed. "Hardly surprising, given what you saw him do." He paused. "So he never once tried to get in touch with you all these years?"

She couldn't understand why that appeared to bother him. "No. Which means he isn't interested in me at all. He's probably all but forgotten me."

"Maybe so, but I guess your subconscious isn't buying it."

In spite of herself, she emitted a short laugh. "Apparently not. I feel so silly sometimes. Nightmares every night? And now a guard dog. That's over-the-top."

He shook his head a little. "I don't think it's over-the-top. Nothing wrong with having a guard dog around, not for anyone. At the very least, Flash will be good company."

She looked down at the dog she was petting. "He sure will be. He's wonderful. Petting him feels good."

"It feels good to him, too. But you'll have to work him every day so he doesn't turn couch potato on you."

Astonishment filled her. "Couch potato? Him?"

"Well, I don't mean he's going to get lazy. But he needs to remain sharp, so every day you're going to have to work with him for at least a half hour. Can you do that?"

"Sure. It'll be fun for both of us."

He smiled. "Good. You'll be a great handler for him. He likes the work, you know. For him it's a fun game. Now let's get busy on the attack training. I'm going to put on my padded suit, and you're going to make him attack me."

She felt perplexed. "But he knows you and likes you! Why would he attack you?"

"Because it doesn't matter that he knows me. Protecting you is all that's going to matter. When you tell him to attack, he'll attack. It's not his job to make decisions like that, but to take care of you. You'll see."

She still hesitated, concerned. "Does he know how to attack?"

"We've been practicing. Now it's time to get serious."

He rose in a single easy movement and went down the run to a shed at the end, disappearing inside. When he returned he wore thick padding on both arms.

Even so, that didn't seem like a whole lot of padding. Flash recognized it immediately and rose to his feet, tail wagging. Dory stood, too.

"He's been practicing on a dummy," Cadell said. "Now he gets the real thing."

They left the run and went out to a paddock, where the two ostriches stared at them over a fence. "Tell him what to do right now," Cadell said mildly.

Dory hesitated, then remembered. "Flash, heel."

The dog immediately came to stand alertly beside her. In all her life, she was sure she had never seen such an incredibly well-behaved dog. He was now still, watchful and right where she wanted him.

"Now you're not going to tell him to attack," Cadell said. "For that I don't like to use such an obvious word, one that he could hear in ordinary speech. It's not only tone that matters. They can pick words right out of a conversation. Now, some dog trainers don't worry about that, but I do. I don't want officers getting in trouble because someone is claiming to have been attacked and the dog reacts somehow."

She nodded, her heart beating nervously. "I understand." But she wasn't at all sure she wanted to command this dog to attack.

"The word I use is *fuss*. Long *u* sound. Like *foos*."

Her sense of humor poked its head up. "I hope I remember that when I need it."

"Well…" His eyes crinkled at the corners. "We'll practice until it becomes natural. But since you're going to start with a very simple command every night when you go to bed, or when you take him out, he'll know what to do even if he doesn't hear the word."

"Meaning?" She began to feel confused.

"If you tell him to guard, he will. And he won't always need an attack command to protect you. He's capable of evaluating a threat that gets too close. This is for when something is a little farther away and he might not see it as a threat to you immediately."

"Ah, okay." Now she was beginning to understand.

He patted her shoulder with his padded mitt. "It's about to all come together. I'm going to walk away about twenty feet. You're going to give the guard command. Then I'm going to turn around and point a toy gun at you. Pay attention to what happens as I approach you."

Okay, she thought. She could do this. "Flash, guard," she said. She felt the dog shift a little beside her but didn't look down at him.

About twenty paces away, Cadell turned around. He held a gun in right hand, but it was pointed down. Flash didn't stir a muscle. Step by step Cadell approached. At ten feet he raised the gun and pointed it at her. Flash didn't need another command. He took off like a shot and bit into the padding on Cadell's right forearm.

"My God," Dory whispered. She'd had no idea. The dog clung to that threatening arm and wouldn't let go even as Cadell tried to shake him off and whirled in circles, lifting Flash's feet from the ground.

"Stop him," Cadell finally said.

"Flash, release," Dory ordered, remembering the

command he had taught her to make the dog drop his toy. Flash obeyed immediately, looking at her. "Heel."

He trotted over to her, looking quite pleased with himself.

"Now the reward," Cadell said.

Which was the yellow tennis ball. She told him he was a good boy as she gave him the ball. Flash chewed on it a few times, then dropped it at her feet, begging for her to throw it, so she did. He raced happily after it.

"It's just that simple," Cadell said, watching her as much as he watched the dog. "A few more steps, a couple of days of practice and he'll do anything for you."

She squatted, encouraging Flash to come back to her. "How do I let him know it's okay not to be on guard?"

"Throw his ball. That means playtime."

So simple, she thought. And so amazingly complex all at the same time. Beautiful, too, she thought as she hugged the Malinois. The dog already made her feel safer. What's more, he made her feel as if she weren't quite as alone.

AFTER DORY LEFT with Betty, Cadell spent the afternoon working with two more officers who were training to become handlers. What they needed was more complex than what Dory needed, and the training was going to take a little longer. Simple fact was, while a civilian could get in some trouble for a misbehaving dog, a cop could have his career ruined. Or the department could be sued. Plus, these guys went into a wider variety of situations, situations that required tracking, rescuing and so on. Dory wouldn't need all those skills.

When he finished that up, he ate a quick dinner, then headed into the sheriff's office to do his shortened shift. On training days, he worked as a deputy for no more than four hours.

Before he left, he took time to feed the ostriches their very expensive feed and open up their pen so they had more room for roaming. Neither of them appeared appreciative.

He and his dog Dasher, also a Malinois, drove into town in his official vehicle and parked near the office. Inside, they found the place quietly humming. Another placid night in Conard County, evidently. He was surprised sometimes how much he enjoyed the relief from the much higher activity level of Seattle. Must be getting old, he thought with an inward smile. Yeah, like thirty-five was ancient.

Dasher settled beside his desk, tucked his nose between his paws and just watched. Since nothing seemed to be happening, he used the computer on his desk to look up the story of Dory Lake and her brother. He felt no qualms about discovering what he could from public records about that incident. He wasn't snooping, but he'd be learning what she had faced and would get a much better threat assessment than Dory's, which seemed to be somewhere between terror and dismissal.

He wasn't surprised to find a twenty-five-year-old case still accessible. The basic police report would be available for many years to come in case George Lake ever got into trouble again. It *was* nice, however, to find it had all been digitized. Newspaper archives were also ready and waiting.

So Dory, just turned seven, had been found screaming in the middle of the street at nearly 2:00 a.m. Neighbors had come running and called the police, who arrived in time to catch George Lake trying to flee the scene. Open-and-shut as far as George was concerned. He'd wiped the murder weapon, but he was far too drenched in blood to claim innocence. For some reason, not clearly explained, he'd been offered a plea bargain for twenty-five years. Drugs appeared to be involved, and the father had been abusive. He guessed the prosecutor couldn't pull together enough to uphold a first-degree murder charge, so George had accepted a bargain down to twenty-five. Without a trial, there was very little in the record to explain any of this.

But what stuck with him was a newspaper account. Apparently, when Dory had stopped screaming, the only words she had said for nearly a year were *red paint*.

God. He sat back in his chair and closed his eyes, seeing it all too clearly. The child had been well and truly traumatized. There was even a mention of hysterical blindness, a conversion disorder, but that hadn't lasted as long as her refusal to speak.

She'd been taken in by her godparents and raised by them, so no additional trauma from foster care, but what difference did that make after what she'd seen? No one, at least in these files, knew exactly how much she had seen, but it was clearly enough to be shrieking in the middle of the road and rendered dumb for nearly a year.

Except for *red paint*.

He'd seen a lot of bad stuff during his career, but the thought of little Dory in the middle of the street… well, the story was enough to break his heart.

As for her mixture of feelings about George…well, that was settled in his mind when he read that Dory had received the entire—very large—insurance payout and all the rest of the property. George might be feeling cheated. In fact, Cadell was inclined to believe he was. He'd lost his entire inheritance because he'd been convicted of killing his parents. He might be thinking he could get some of that back. Make Dory pay him to leave her alone.

Or maybe worse. Because it occurred to him that if Dory died, her only heir would be her brother…and if he weren't linked to her death…

Hell. He switched over to the reports menu and tried to shake the ugly feelings.

Being a cop had made him a much more suspicious man by nature. Sometimes he had to pull himself back and take a colder view, stifle his feelings and use his brain.

But his gut was telling him this wasn't good at all.

DORY WAS ALL excited about Flash when she saw Betty again that afternoon. "I feel like a kid at Christmas," she confided. "That dog is wonderful. I fell in love instantly."

Betty laughed and poured the coffee. "I knew a dog was a good idea. He'll brighten your days even if you never need him."

"I need him already," Dory admitted. "I'm so used to living in a world that exists only on my computer I'd forgotten a few other things might be nice. A friend like you, a dog like Flash."

"A man like Cadell," Betty remarked casually.

It took a second for Dory to catch on. "Betty! Are you trying to matchmake?"

"Never." Betty grinned at her. "I just meant you should give him a chance to be a friend. He's been in town for a year now, and I haven't heard anything but kind words about him. So I'm fairly certain you can trust him…as a friend. But I ought to warn you— grapevine has it that he had a messy divorce and he doesn't even date."

Dory shifted uncomfortably. She was well aware that Betty felt she cut herself off too much from the real world. And not just because of her job.

But trust didn't come easily to her. It hadn't since that night. It had even taken her godparents a while to get past the barriers that had slammed in place back then. If she hadn't already known and loved them, it might never have happened. Betty was the unique exception, worming her way past ice and stone and into Dory's heart.

"I'll try, Betty," she said eventually. "But I tend

to get stubborn if I feel pushed." And anyway, she hadn't missed Betty's warning about Cadell's aversion to women. Which suited her fine.

"Tell me about it, girl." Then Betty laughed. "No pushing. Just saying Cadell's a nice guy and you can trust him. I'd never advise you to reach for more than that. Anyway, I've got some women friends you'd probably like, too, but you notice I haven't invited them over since you arrived."

Instantly Dory felt ashamed. "I'm sorry. I don't want to disrupt your life. You should just keep living the way you always do. If I get uncomfortable, I can take a walk. And I'll be in my new place soon. I can go tonight if you want."

Betty sat straight up. "What makes you think I want you to go? Cut it out. I love having you here. Anyway, you're not moving until Cadell gives you a dog." Pause. "When is George getting out?"

"Tomorrow, I think. Or maybe the next day." She looked down. "You'd think the date would be engraved in my memory, considering what it's doing to me."

Betty's face tightened. "Then you're definitely staying with me. You need someone around when the nightmares disturb you. Maybe the dog will help once you have him. I hope so. But in the meantime, you're not going anywhere."

"They're just dreams," Dory protested, although neither her heart nor her gut entirely believed it. Her brother was a living, breathing monster, not some fantasy creature. She might never see him again. In fact, she hoped she never did. But as long as she was alive, he rode in the cold seas of her memory, a very real threat.

Later, as she helped Betty make dinner, she made up her mind. She was moving tomorrow. She'd dealt with the nightmares all her life. Maybe not as bad as they were right now, but she'd dealt with them. She could continue to deal with them.

But she wasn't going to turn Betty into some kind of shut-in for her own benefit. No way. The woman had a life here and deserved to enjoy it. As for herself, well, even though George might be released tomorrow, there was no possible way for him to get here tomorrow. Or even the next day.

And she still couldn't imagine any reason why he'd ever want to see her again. They'd been close when she was little. He'd held her on his lap and read to her to distract her from their parents' fighting. But that had been a very long time ago. After twenty-five years, there was nothing left to put back together. Nothing.

Besides, whoever she had thought her brother was when she was little, he'd shattered all that one night in the kitchen. No way those shards would ever fit together again.

In the morning she drove herself out to Cadell's ranch for another training session. Betty had a meeting to attend, but having been to the ranch once, Dory didn't have any trouble finding the place. She loved driving down the battered county roads in the open places, looking at the mountains that appeared to jut up suddenly from nowhere. The land rolled, hinting at foothills, but these mountains looked as if they had been dropped there, not developed slowly over eons. Maybe that was just perspective, but she stored it in her mind for use someday in her art.

Cadell was waiting for her when she pulled up. He sat in a rocker on his wide front porch and stood immediately. The day was exquisite, Dory thought as she climbed out of her car. Warm but not hot, tickled by a gentle breeze. The kind of day where it was possible just to feel good to be alive.

"Howdy," he said from the top of the steps. Today he wore a long-sleeved tan work shirt, sleeves rolled up, and jeans. "You want to get straight to work or do you have time for some coffee first?"

He probably wanted coffee himself, and while she *was* in a hurry, wanting to get her move taken care of during the afternoon, she decided to be polite. The man was doing her a big favor, after all.

Inside, his house was welcoming, showing signs that he was doing some renovation.

"Excuse my mess," he said as they went to the kitchen. "My dad kind of let things go the last few years, and I couldn't get away for long enough to really take this place in hand."

"I don't mind. So you grew up here?"

"Yup. Left when I was twenty for the law enforcement academy, then I took a job in Seattle."

She sat at the table and watched him as he moved

around digging out mugs and pouring coffee. Man, was he built. She wished he'd just sit down so her eyes wouldn't be drawn like a magnet.

"This must seem awfully tame after Seattle."

"I like that part." Smiling, he brought her coffee. Sugar and milk were already on the table. "I get to spend more time with the dogs."

"And ostriches," she dared to tease.

He laughed and sat across from her. "And ostriches," he agreed.

"So no idea how they came to be here?"

He shook his head. "Dad had enough time to set up the electrified fencing, but the vet, Mike Windwalker, tells me he only had them a couple of months before he passed. Mike had no idea where they came from, either—Dad just asked for his advice on keeping them healthy. Once. I wish he'd mentioned them when we talked on the phone, but he never did."

"Maybe he thought he wouldn't have them for long."

He shook his head a little. "Possible, I suppose, but that fencing...well, yeah, he'd have needed to do something quick to keep them from escaping. I'd love to know where they came from, but when I ask around, nobody seems to know a thing."

A smile suddenly split his face. "In a way it was funny. I got the call that Dad had passed, and as I was packing to get out here, I got a second call that left me floored. It was from Mike, the vet. He said he'd take care of the ostriches for a few days so not to worry. I'm standing there holding the phone with my jaw dropped. Ostriches?"

A giggle escaped Dory. "That'd be a shocker."

"Believe it. And I was no less shocked when I got here and found out how ornery they are." He paused. "Okay, maybe that's just my feeling and I ought to give them more of a chance. But they've already killed two of my favorite hats, and I don't much like being pecked whenever they feel like it. I'm hoping we can eventually reach a truce."

She glanced out his window and saw the two ostriches in the small pen not far away. They weren't especially cuddly looking, even now when they were just looking around. "Are they hard to care for?"

"I have to special-order feed for them. One of the big pet food companies also makes food for zoos, so that helps. Special ostrich blend. And in the winter when it gets too cold, I need to keep them in the barn."

"So they don't have to be in a warm climate all the time?"

"Evidently not." He sighed, half smiling, an attractive man comfortable in his own skin. She envied him that. Had she ever felt comfortable within herself, apart from her work? "I really would like to give them to someone who actually wants them."

"Wants them as pets?"

"Not likely. As far as I can tell, they weren't hand raised as babies. Or maybe they just don't like me." He shrugged. "But I won't sell them for meat or leather. Betty keeps reminding me that ostriches are worth thousands of dollars, but I'm not looking for that. There's a market for their eggs, though, a very expensive market, so I'm just trying to find someone who wants them for that, or for breeding. Although some days I think they'd make fine boots."

She laughed, delighted by his self-deprecating humor. "Are they really troublesome?"

He leaned back, turning his coffee cup slowly on the table with one hand. "In all fairness, no. If they were parakeet-sized, they'd be cool. They're not doing a darn thing birds don't do. They're just doing it in a *much* bigger way."

She laughed again. "I had a parakeet when I was ten. You have my sympathy. My bird liked to peck."

"These like to peck, too. It can be painful."

"And costly in terms of hats, you said?"

"Two of my favorites, gone." He suddenly grinned. "Come on, let's go work with Flash."

Her own eagerness surprised her, but it shouldn't have. Since she awoke this morning, she'd been impatient to see Flash again. She was already coming to love that dog, she realized. She hoped Cadell judged her ready to take him with her soon.

Then it struck her: she had no way yet to care for Flash. No food, no bowls, no bed, no leash...wow. She needed to take care of that fast.

She mentioned that to Cadell as they stepped out back through his mudroom. "I feel silly for not taking care of it yesterday."

He shook his head. "Every dog here has his own

bowls and leashes, and they go with him. Same with his favorite toy. As for a bed…he'll sleep just about anywhere you let him, but I'm warning you, if you invite him onto the bed, he may claim possession."

That elicited another laugh from her, and amazement wafted through her again. She hadn't felt this good since she got the news about George. Her spirits were up, her confidence was high—all because of one dog trainer and a dog named Flash.

She wondered how long that would last.

He paused halfway to the dog run and faced her. "You can love him, Dory. Just don't spoil him. Remember, he's a working dog, and working makes him happy. Keep his training fresh and establish your boundaries. Then you'll have a great relationship."

She nodded and followed him, thinking that was probably good advice for people, too.

Flash's tail wagged fast, and she could have sworn he grinned at her as they approached. Excited or not, however, he didn't misbehave, and when released from his kennel, he merely nosed her hand in greeting. Dory, however, was a little more exuberant, squatting to rub his neck and sides. "You're a beautiful boy," she heard herself saying. Talking to a dog?

But as she looked into Flash's warm brown eyes, it suddenly felt right. She suspected this dog understood more than she would ever know.

She looked up at Cadell and found him smiling affectionately down at her and the dog. "Okay," he said, "let's go. Maybe you can take him home with you today."

CADELL REALIZED HE was developing a problem. His attraction to Dory wouldn't quit. Yes, she'd caught his eye with her almost ethereal beauty, but that should have worn off quickly. It wasn't as if she was the only beautiful woman he had ever seen.

No, something about her was reaching deeper than mere superficial attraction, and that wasn't good. He had years of experience in a lousy marriage to teach him that even cop groupies didn't necessarily like being married to a cop. The endless complaints that had assaulted him after the first six months of marriage should have been lesson enough. If something kept him late and he missed dinner, an explosion would result. If he had to break a date because of his job, he found no understanding. Sometimes he'd wondered if the woman would be glad if he never came home from one of his shifts.

It wasn't his safety that had worried her. No, she was annoyed that his job interfered with her life, and that was not a happy way to live, for either of them.

In the process he'd learned that love could die fast with the wrong person, and that was painful all by itself. Since his divorce, finally agreed to when the fighting became almost constant after a few years, he'd avoided entanglements. He didn't know whether he was guilty of lousy judgment—although as a cop his judgment was usually pretty good—or whether he was just poison. Brenda had turned into a woman he didn't recognize, and he wondered if that was his doing.

Anyway, even in his new job the unexpected happened. A search for a missing person could keep him from home for days, often without warning. And that was only one example. So…he judged it best to avoid long-term affairs. Maybe later in life, he told himself. Maybe when he retired from being a cop and devoted himself to the dog-training school he was slowly starting. Maybe after he got rid of those dang ostriches.

He enjoyed helping Dory run Flash through his paces, though. As the sun rose higher, with frequent breaks for Flash to lap water, he watched the woman and dog bond more securely. From his perspective, Flash had totally given his loyalty to Dory. He was already crazy about her.

There was no better protection than that. But there was still her brother. Unease niggled at Cadell. While a trained dog was great, it wasn't a perfect solution. There were always ways around a dog if you thought about it—usually a bullet.

When they were done with training and Dory sat on the hard ground to play tug with Flash for a little while, Cadell dropped beside her and stretched out, propping himself on an elbow.

"You ever marry?" he asked, mainly because if she told him she'd had a lousy marriage he could hope she'd have as many reasons to avoid involvement as he had. One thing for sure—with this woman he was going to need a lot of protection for himself. Everything about her appealed to him.

"No," she answered as she threw the knotted rope and Flash leaped into the air to catch it. Her reply was remarkable in its brevity. Interestingly, she didn't ask him, which would have been the usual conversational flow.

He decided to plunge in anyway. An understated warning to both of them. "I was," he said.

Her attention returned to him as Flash brought the rope back to her and dropped it in her lap. "Flash, down," she said. All of this was coming naturally to her, and he smiled. Flash obeyed immediately, head still high and curious. "Not good?" she asked.

"Awful," he said frankly.

"I'm sorry."

He wondered if he should tell her more, then decided to go for it. She'd gotten his attention enough in so many ways that he was going to be checking up on her frequently. Officer Friendly, as long as George might be a threat.

"My wife, Brenda, was a cop groupie." He watched her eyes widen. "Now, a smart cop knows that's dangerous, that most of those women just want a notch on the headboard. But Brenda seemed different. Maybe she was. I never heard of her sleeping with any of the other guys. But she used to sit there in the bar with big eyes, encouraging us to talk, basking in as much of the camaraderie as we were willing to share with her."

Dory nodded slowly. "I'm picturing it, but probably all wrong."

"Probably not. Some women love the uniform, not what's inside it. And some cops want brief affairs and one-night stands, just like the women. Consenting adults and all that. But Brenda seemed different. Unfortunately, she was."

Dory looked down and scratched Flash behind one ear. "How so?"

"I felt drawn to her, so I started sitting with her more and more often. As we got to know each other better, I decided she was genuine and I liked her. So we started dating. Long story short, I fell in love, we got married, and six months later I started to learn how wrong I was."

He plucked a blade of dried grass, shaking his head, then stared away from her out over the pasture to the nearby mountains. He'd had mountains in Seattle, but here…these were already special to him somehow.

"Anyway, it turned out she couldn't stand my job. Irregular hours, broken plans. She started in on me for being unreliable, demanding I find a regular job."

She drew an audible breath. "She called a police officer unreliable? Really?"

"In all fairness, from her perspective I probably was. I lost count of the times I missed dinner or a movie date with her. She wanted a very different kind of life, and I wanted to remain in law enforcement. So then it got truly ugly. No reason to rake it up. But I learned something."

"Yes?"

He looked up and found her blue eyes on him. "That maybe I should just avoid marrying anyone. I sure as hell was doing something wrong, something I never seemed able to fix unless I gave up part of myself."

Now it was her turn to look away toward the mountains. Whatever she was thinking, Flash sensed something and stirred a bit, raising his gaze to her face. Almost instinctively, she petted him.

"I never got that close to anyone," she said after a minute or two. "I couldn't tell you whether either or both of you were at fault."

"I'm not asking for that," he said quickly. "But since we're probably going to be seeing each other quite a bit because of Flash, I thought…"

"We could be friends," she finished for him. She turned her face toward him. "I don't make friends, Cadell. Except for Betty. She's the lone exception." She closed her eyes briefly, then snapped them open. "I'm incapable of real trust. Even years of therapy didn't help with that. So…consider me broken, which I guess I am."

Then she rose to her feet. Flash stood, too.

Cadell gave up on trying to reach her. He'd issued the warning he'd wanted to, but evidently she didn't need it.

Closed up, walled in, all because of something she saw as a child. He wished he could say that surprised him.

He stood, too. "Want to take Flash home with you today?"

"Betty's cats might object."

"I thought you were moving?"

"I almost decided to, then changed my mind. Tomorrow, when the internet is installed."

Everything settled, returning to normal. Back to business. "Okay," he said. "I'll keep him for you and bring him over tomorrow."

Flash wanted to go with her when she started toward her car, but she told him to stay. Looking forlorn, he settled on his belly and put his snout between his paws.

Dory didn't miss the expression. "Tomorrow, Flash. I promise."

Cadell watched her drive away, forgetting himself and standing too close to the penned ostriches. He ducked just in time and stepped away.

"Dang birds," he said, but his mind was elsewhere. He'd just learned a lot about Dory Lake, and far from putting him off, it made him hurt for her.

Damn her brother. If that guy showed up in this county, Cadell was going to feed him to the birds. The big birds.

Chapter Three

The next morning, Betty insisted on helping Dory move many of her belongings. Most of it was computer equipment, some very heavy, but Betty brought the clothes and lighter items for the kitchen.

The house was partially furnished, which made Dory's life easier, and already contained the items she'd had shipped here, mostly work related office furniture, including the extra battered old chair that tipped back farther than the new one. She loved to sit in it sometimes just to think. Eventually she could spiff the house or her office up if she wanted, but with most of her attention on her job, on creating graphics with her team, she was seldom more than half-aware of her surroundings.

The pile of clothes on her bed amused Betty, however. Jeans. T-shirts. More jeans. Sweatshirts. "Lord, girl, don't you ever dress up?"

"I don't have any need." But Dory laughed, too. It did look odd, all together like that. Add the plain undies and the three pairs of jogging shoes and she was sure she would appall most women.

"We have to do something about your fashion sense," Betty remarked.

"Why?" Dory asked. And that really *was* the question. She worked long days, she had no desire to socialize and the one man who'd managed to pierce her desire for isolation had told her he wasn't interested because he'd had a bad marriage. She didn't need a neon sign.

Betty followed her into her office and watched as Dory unpacked the real center of her life. "You know I love you," she said as Dory pulled out the first of six monitors.

"I know." She braced herself for what she was certain was coming.

"You need more of a life than your job. Won't you at least meet one or two people I think you'd like?"

"I met Cadell," she reminded Betty. "Nice guy. Also seriously burned by life."

Betty sighed, then said a bit sarcastically, "Well, at least you're a pair, then."

"Nope," said Dory. "Nice and all that, great dog trainer…"

"And gorgeous as hell," Betty said bluntly. "At least tell me you're not blind."

Dory paused, a power cord in her hand. "Betty? Please tell me you're not going to keep pushing me this way. Because if that's your goal, I'll stop unpacking right now."

The room nearly turned to ice as Betty stared at her. Then almost as quickly as it came, the ice thawed. "No, that's not my goal. I just worry about you. None of my business, I guess."

Betty turned and went to get some more items from the car. Dory stared after her, realizing she had just hurt her only friend in the world.

Well, take that as a warning, she told herself. All

she brought was pain. Whatever lay at her core, it was locked away forever. And that hurt other people.

She returned to setting up her office, glad to know that soon she'd been in touch with her team, the nerds who were fun and smart and never demanded she get personal about anything. A meeting of minds. Who needed a meeting of hearts?

As she turned back to her desk and began to connect more cables, she felt herself easing back into her comfortable world where she could control everything she needed to. Even her desk, shipped from her old home, seemed like a warm greeting, encouraging a new life.

Her life. Then she thought of Flash. Okay, so maybe there was more to it than the digital world she lived in.

Betty returned, her voice announcing her. She was speaking with someone, and Dory instinctively stiffened. She pivoted quickly to see Betty enter the office space with a woman wearing a tool belt.

"Dory, this is Rhonda, your cable man."

Rhonda laughed. "I'm your cable tech person."

Dory couldn't help grinning. "You get that, too?"

"All the time. Say, I hear you're into graphics design?"

Dory nodded.

"Then I'll make sure you have the best connection this company can offer. I'm a gamer. So what graphics cards do you use?"

Betty rolled her eyes. "I'll go get the last few things, then make some coffee. I can see what's coming."

Dory and Rhonda both laughed but soon were involved in the nuts and bolts of computing and bandwidth and a whole range of technical subjects. While they gabbed, Rhonda busied herself putting the connectors in the wall, testing them and then adding the routers. "The best we have," she said, placing the two routers on the desk. "Betty kind of rattled some bars, you know? So you'll have two broadband connections. That's what you wanted, right?"

"As long as they're not piggybacking and sucking up the bandwidth from each other."

"I'll take care of that at the junction outside. It's wonderful how far we're coming. A federal grant is making it possible, you know. High-speed connections in rural areas. You wouldn't have been able to stand it here a few years ago. We were still with the dinosaurs and dial-up."

"Oh, man, dial-up was a nightmare."

Rhonda finished quickly, considering all she had to do inside, including hooking up Dory's TV and converter box, and that was just the beginning. A lot more to do outside. But she took time for a quick cup of coffee with Dory and Betty before getting to it.

"Hope to see you again," she said cheerfully to Dory before she zipped out the door.

"Nice woman," Dory remarked and went back screwing, snapping, plugging and otherwise turning a collection of expensive hardware into two expensive, smoothly running workstations. Everything top-of-the-line. The max.

At last, though, she was able to turn everything on

and test it. All good. She sent an email blast letting her team know she was back on the grid. Almost immediately her computer pinged with the arrival of emails.

She was home.

CADELL LEFT FOR work a couple of hours early, carting two dogs with him, Flash and Dasher. Dasher was eager to get to work, recognizing the backseat cage of the sheriff's department SUV as the beginning of adventure. Flash didn't see it that way, but he was glad to take a car ride.

He hoped he didn't unnerve Dory, dressed as he was in his khaki uniform, gun belt and tan Stetson. Not the guy she was used to seeing in shirts with rolled-up sleeves and jeans.

He pulled into Dory's driveway, behind a blue Honda sedan that had seen better years. The house was small and old in the way of many in this part of town, but it had been recently painted white. The driveway was two wheel paths of concrete, the sidewalk cracked but not heaving yet, and the porch from a time when porches were inviting.

Not that Dory would probably care about that. Betty had mentioned that Dory wasn't very sociable, and that she worried about her being too deeply mired in her work.

Being mired in work was something Cadell understood perfectly, so he didn't hold that against her. Given the woman's background, he wasn't even surprised that she had told him she couldn't trust. He figured Flash would be the best therapy he could offer her. Dogs had a way of getting past defenses.

He left Dasher in the car with the engine running so the air-conditioning would keep him cool and walked Flash on a leash to the front door.

"Your new home, Flash. You take good care of it."

He knocked. There was a doorbell, but cops never used them and the habit was impossible to break. At least he didn't use the heel of his fist or his big flashlight to resound through the house. A normal type of knock that shouldn't startle her.

A couple of minutes passed while he looked around the neighborhood and wondered if she had decided to take a walk. Clearly her car was here.

Then the door opened, and Dory was blinking at him. "Oh! You look so different in uniform, I almost didn't recognize you. I'm sorry, I forgot you were coming this afternoon."

He smiled. "Not a problem. If you want to take Flash's leash, I'll go get his supplies. Can't stay— my dog's in the car, and while it's specially built with heavy-duty air-conditioning to keep him cool…well, I never trust it too far."

He hesitated, holding the leash out to her. She bit her lower lip, then blurted, "Can you bring Dasher inside, too?"

He glanced at his watch and saw that he still had plenty of time to grab a bite at Maude's Diner and get to the station. "Sure. It might help Flash feel a little more at home."

She smiled then, a faint smile, but it reached her eyes as she accepted the leash. "These dogs are practically people to you," she remarked.

He had turned and now looked over his shoulder. "Nah. They're nicer than a lot of people."

That made her laugh quietly, and the sound followed him as he went to turn off his vehicle and get Dasher. He liked her, he realized. It wasn't just that she was beautiful. Oh, hell, he didn't need the trouble.

But he brought Dasher inside anyway and left him with Dory while he returned to the back of his car. Two bowls, a large padded bed, several tennis balls, chew toys and forty pounds of dry dog food later, he was sitting at her rickety kitchen table, watching her search her fridge for a soft drink to give him.

"So it's true computer types drink a lot of soda?" he asked casually.

"As long as it has caffeine. I can do a good job with a pot of coffee, as well. Orange, cola or lime?"

"Orange," he decided. "Cheetos?"

"Now that's a stereotype too far," she said with humor as she passed him the bottle of soda. Evidently it didn't come with a glass in her world. "Although," she said as she slid into the one other chair, "I did have a friend in college who loved to eat them sometimes, but she didn't like the grit on her keyboard. So she ate them with chopsticks."

The image drew a hearty laugh from him, and her smile deepened.

She spoke again. "Thanks for bringing all the doggy

stuff. You never said, but how much do I owe you? You're giving me a well-trained guard dog that you must have spent a lot of time on."

He shook his head slowly. "I'm kinda thinking of Flash as an extension of my oath to serve and protect. He's a gift, Dory, if that won't offend you."

Her eyes widened. "But, Cadell…"

"No *but*s. You can be my advertising around town, how's that?"

Both dogs, trailing their leads, were sniffing their way around the house, checking out everything. Dory watched them for several minutes, the faint smile still on her face. After a bit she said, "I've never received a better gift."

"I hope you'll never need his finer skills."

"Me, too."

Silence fell. He glanced at his watch and saw he had a little longer. Somehow it didn't feel right to just walk out.

Then Dory surprised him by asking, "What else do you teach the dogs to do? There must be a lot involved in police work."

"Apart from what we taught Flash to do? Plenty. A dog has a wonderful nose, hundreds of times more sensitive than ours. It can follow scents that are weeks old, and even those that are high in the air. That's an extremely useful tool in searching, particularly search and rescue."

"Do you do a lot of search and rescue?"

"Around here? In the mountains, quite enough. Hikers, mainly. Then there are elderly people who sometimes ramble and forget where they are. Earlier this summer we had to hunt for an autistic girl. She'd wandered off, become frightened and hid in a culvert out of sight."

"Her parents must have been terrified. My word, *she* must have been terrified!"

He smiled. "She didn't trust us, but she trusted the dog."

He watched her smile again. For a woman who had come here to escape a possible threat, and who, according to Betty, suffered from a lot of nightmares, she smiled easily. Props to her, he thought.

"Anyway," he continued, "it's possible to train the dogs to hunt only for specific scents, too. Like explosives. Or drugs. Or cadavers."

Her smile faded. "Dead tissue?"

"We train them to distinguish human tissue from animal tissue, and their success rate is about ninety-five percent. They can find buried bodies a century old. And they can smell them down to at least fifteen feet, and some say up to thirty."

Her eyes had grown wider. "So they don't get confused?"

"No." But he didn't want to get into the details. Some things just didn't need to be talked about.

She looked down, then lifted her head and drank from her own bottle of orange soda. "How do they learn all this stuff? I mean, isn't it hard to teach them?"

"A little patience and they pick it up pretty quickly.

They're remarkable, and they're eager to please."
Dasher came over and laid his head on Cadell's thigh.
"I think he's ready to go to work."

Dory popped to her feet immediately. "I'm sorry,
I've been holding you up."

"Actually, no. I allowed some extra time." He
reached into his breast pocket and pulled out a folded
slip of paper. "Feeding directions and all that. If you
have any questions, call me. And if you don't mind,
I'll drop by every day or so to see how you two are
getting on."

Holding the paper, she looked at him. "I'll never be
able to thank you enough, Cadell."

He chuckled. "Tell me that again when you have fur
all over the place. He doesn't shed a lot, but he's going
to shed. See you tomorrow afternoon."

He headed for the door with Dasher and heard Dory
behind him telling Flash to stay. The dog needed to
learn his new home. He figured Dory was going to
make it easy on him.

As he climbed into his vehicle with Dasher in the
cage behind him, he realized something. Betty unin-
tentionally had painted Dory unfairly. She might not
be prepared to trust people and allow them within her
circle; she might be scared to death of her brother's
imminent release from prison; she might be haunted
by terrible nightmares.

But Dory had grit. Real inner strength.

He liked her. He respected her. And he needed to

watch his step, because he sure as hell didn't ever want to make another woman miserable.

DORY AND FLASH regarded each other in the kitchen. She'd removed his leash, but he sat there staring up at her as if he were pleading.

She tapped the piece of paper Cadell had given her. "It says here you don't get supper for another two hours."

Flash lowered his head a bit.

Feeling like the wicked witch, Dory scanned the paper again. "But you can have your dental chew. What the heck is that?"

She looked at the heap of supplies in one corner of her kitchen, then rose to look through it. She discovered a plastic bag behind the huge bag of food. In it was a nubby nylon or plastic bone of some kind. Unzipping the bag, she pulled it out and turned to hold it out to Flash. "Is this what you want?"

He stared at it and licked his lips.

There could be a minor problem with a dog so well trained, she thought. Was he just going to sit there like a statue or let her know what he wanted? "Take it, Flash," she said finally in desperation.

He apparently understood that. In one leap he reached the bone and took it from her hand with amazing delicacy before settling down to gnaw on it.

"Well, cool," she said. "We have communication!"

Flash barely glanced at her. Almost grinning, she sat down at the table to read the directions from Cadell more carefully. From the other room she heard her email dinging, but she ignored it. Flash was more important.

She nearly giggled when she read what Cadell had typed at the top of the page: *The care and feeding of your personal K-9.* She wondered if he gave that to all his trainees.

Flash looked up at her, forgetting his bone for a few seconds as he wagged his tail at her. He seemed so happy right now, it was impossible not to feel the same.

LATER, AFTER SHE had caught up on email and re-opened her participation in the project, she felt a nose gently prod her thigh. A glance at the clock told her it was after eleven…and she hadn't walked Flash since he arrived.

She put her conference on hold, explaining she needed to walk her dog. Hoping she didn't get the slew of jokes she half expected, she found Flash's leash. The dog gave one joyful bark, then stood perfectly still while she hooked it to his collar.

That was when it struck her how late it was. Ordinarily she worked well into the night, but before she hadn't been afraid of anything. Now she was afraid. Her brother might already be out of prison. They'd given her the exact date, but she'd run the letter through the shredder as soon as the shock had passed. She wanted nothing with his name on it.

So today. Maybe tomorrow, but most probably today.

Betty knew for sure because Dory had told her, but it was too late to call and verify it.

Point was…she was suddenly frightened of the night and its secrets, a fear she hadn't felt in a long time.

She looked at Flash and saw him watching her, not a muscle twitching. He must have felt her abrupt burst of dread.

"I shouldn't be silly about this," she said aloud, not entirely believing herself. "I have you, after all."

The slightest wag of Flash's tail. God, the dog seemed to be reading her like an open book. Could he do that?

"I promised to take good care of you. I'm sorry I didn't walk you sooner, but do you think you could manage with just a short trip to the backyard?"

He looked agreeable, but he probably didn't understand a word of her prattle. God, she had grown so completely unnerved for no good reason. George, even if he wanted to find her, couldn't have located her yet. She hadn't even needed to leave a forwarding address, because she paid all her bills online and the rest was junk. She'd established no real connections here yet except the broadband and that didn't have her full name on it. She was truly off the grid as far as the world was concerned.

She would be very hard to find, she assured herself as she began to walk toward the back door. "Flash, heel," she said quietly, and he walked right beside her.

Besides, she had a guard dog. Flash would make George's life hell. So she was safe, yeah?

She just wished she could believe it.

The night beyond the door felt pregnant with threat. But it was the same backyard that had been there when she rented the place. With a locked six-foot wooden privacy fence around it. She'd know if anybody tried to get past that.

And there was Flash, of course. Oddly, however, as impressed as she was by the dog, she didn't know if she was prepared to put her life in his paws.

God, she was losing it. Stiffening her back, she pulled the door open and let herself out with the dog. Should she unleash him?

But Flash seemed to be reading the situation well. As soon as they reached grass near a shrub, he did his business, then turned around to face the house again. He sensed she wanted to get back behind locked doors.

Tonight she was in no mood to disagree, or to even try to reason through her probably unreasonable fear. Just get back inside and give Flash a treat. Tomorrow in the daylight she could give him a longer walk, even work with him.

But not tonight. She felt as if evil lurked out there, and she didn't want to find out if she was right.

GEORGE NEEDED MONEY to travel. Everything else was on hold until he had more than the pittance he'd received at his release late that afternoon, fourteen hours earlier than he'd expected. But then, he'd been a model prisoner, and he noticed they'd dated the paperwork for the next morning.

But he didn't have enough money to travel on or eat while he figured out exactly how he was going to deal with Dory. The bus ticket they'd given him was nonrefundable, meant only to take him back to the place where he'd originally lived—a small suburb of Saint Louis.

He'd been given the address of a halfway house, so he went there, arriving late at night, and resigned himself to spending some time figuring out how to get his hands on some money quickly. He sure as hell didn't intend to work any of the low-paying menial jobs they probably would point him to. He had bigger things to hunt.

Even though it was late, with his release papers he got inside the door. They showed him to a bedroom and didn't seem particularly worried that he asked to use a computer. The residents had one in a public room downstairs. Help himself.

So he did. He was too keyed up to just go to sleep. He'd dozed on the bus anyway. The only thing about this that shocked him was his surprising discomfort at not being surrounded by walls when he'd walked from the bus to this place. Not having his every movement watched or directed.

He'd never imagined the world could feel so big, and he suspected that once tomorrow began and life resumed out there, it was going to overwhelm him with chaos. He wasn't used to chaos anymore. The order of his days had become deeply embedded over twenty-five years.

But so had sitting at a computer and hunting for information about his sister. She had vanished from the town where she had grown up. She was reputed to be a partner in a graphics business that had no address other than a web URL and email. The godparents who had raised her were dead.

He needed to know more about her than this, but he suspected if he called people around here in their old hometown he'd meet a brick wall. Well, unless he could somehow convince them he was someone else. Not likely. He feared too many local people might remember him. Maybe not young people, but the older ones who had probably devoured all the lurid details in the newspaper and on the evening news.

With that thought in mind, he headed upstairs to his room, where his bed was ready to be made. His own room. It had been a while. Not big, but bigger than a cell, without a cell mate.

For a little while the space bothered him, but then he settled down. Room was a good thing. If he thought back very hard to his early days in the slammer, he remembered how claustrophobic he had felt. No more of that.

Now there was infinite freedom.

He needed to remember how to enjoy it. To use it.

Chapter Four

Dan Casey dropped by Cadell's place in the morning. Dan had recently married a woman with a young daughter and was now expecting an addition to the family. Fellow deputies, he and Cadell had built a good friendship.

"So," said Dan, pausing near the ostrich pen. The birds had been let out into the larger corral but didn't seem interested in taking advantage of the space. They regarded Dan with the same glare they gave Cadell. Dan shook his head.

"So?" Cadell asked.

"Krys wants to come out and see the birds," Dan remarked, referring to his five-year-old stepdaughter.

"Krys would be snack-sized for those demons," Cadell said with a wink. "Bring her anytime I'm home."

"And then there's the puppy she wants."

"Ah. Come on in, if you have time. Is she thinking young puppy? The vet has plenty for adoption."

"I know." Dan shrugged. "She likes the police dogs."

A chuckle escaped Cadell. "You're in for it. And I don't mean from the dog."

"I didn't figure."

They walked into the house together. The morning's coffee had just finished brewing, so Cadell poured a couple of cups and they settled at his trestle table, left over from the days when hired hands ate with the family.

Cadell asked, "So what's happening with Krys and what does her mother think?"

"Well, that's the other question. Vicki has mixed feelings. She thinks a dog would teach Krys some responsibility but that in the end the two of us would be taking care of most of it. The idea of a puppy is irresistible, but every time Vicki mentions it, Krys gets a very mulish look and says she wants a police dog."

Cadell nodded slowly. "Her birth father was a cop, wasn't he?"

"Yeah, and Vicki's wondering how much that has to do with this. It's hard to tell, but maybe Krys has some lingering fears because of her father's death."

Cadell pondered that as he sipped his first cup of coffee for the day. A lot more would probably follow. "Well, I can give her a well-trained dog that would protect her and obey her. But you or Vicki are going to have to keep the training fresh or you'll wind up with just another dog. Which might be okay."

Dan sighed and rapped his fingers on the table. "The problem is, Krys isn't being very clear about exactly what she means by a police dog. Does she just want to know it's a police dog? Does she want it to be able to do certain things? One thing for sure, I am not giving that child a dog that will attack on command."

Cadell had to laugh. "I wouldn't dream of it. A kid that young? One temper tantrum…"

"Exactly." Dan grinned. "I don't think she'd tell the dog to hold us at bay, but by the time she's a teen that could change."

Both men laughed then.

Cadell spoke as his laughter faded. "I can make sure the dog recognizes certain people as friends, no problem. And I can train it to protect her without an attack command." He paused and lifted one brow. "You *do* understand that if the dog perceives a threat to her, he *will* attack without a command?"

Dan frowned. "Depends on what kind of threat. I mean, the mailman holding out an envelope…"

Cadell shook his head. "No, more like a stranger takes her by her arm or hand. Or tries to get her in a car. Come on, Dan, you've worked with these dogs before. You must have some idea of how well they can discriminate."

"Most of the ones I've worked with haven't been that finely tuned. I didn't know if they could be. So, okay. I'll leave it to you."

Cadell hesitated. "Wait a sec. I have an idea. I just gave a guard dog to a new friend in town."

"Dory Lake? I heard about her from Betty, I think it was." Dan was suddenly all cop. "What's the problem?"

"Her older brother killed their parents. He just finished a twenty-five-year sentence, and Dory is naturally nervous about him being on the loose again." He didn't offer anything more than that. Not his place. Dan could look up the same files, if he wanted to.

Dan frowned. "She might have a reason to be worried." Then he returned to the subject at hand. "So what's your idea?"

"I just thought that with Dory's permission maybe you and Vicki and I could bring Krys to see Dory's dog, Flash. He's a youngster, just two, and trained only to protect. Krys might discover she wants something very different."

"I like that idea," Dan agreed. "It might settle Vicki some, too. I think she's concerned about putting a potentially lethal K-9 in the hands of a five-year-old."

"I wouldn't do that," Cadell said. "I hope you know that. But I'd really like to meet Krys again and talk about it. See if we can find out what's going on in the child's head."

"I'd love to know that, too. It's not like her dad was a K-9 handler. I don't know where this came from. But," Dan said with a shrug, "I often don't know where Krys gets some of her ideas. She's a mystery at times."

AROUND TWO THAT AFTERNOON, Dory stretched and turned off her computer monitors, allowing her recent construct for the graphics scene to render into a high-definition, nearly realistic image. It wouldn't take long, given the power and number of graphics cards she had, but it did remind her that she needed to take Flash on a longer walk than just around her backyard. She'd also promised to work with him to keep him fresh.

Perfect time to do her part by the dog and grab something to eat, maybe a sandwich. She and Betty had stocked her freezer with easy-to-prepare foods, although Betty had tsked quite a bit and said Dory had to promise to come over every Sunday for a decent meal.

Amused, shaking her head, she said aloud, "Flash, walk."

She heard the scrabble of his claws on the wood floor in the hall, and by the time she reached the front door he was standing there with his leash in his mouth.

Smart dog, she thought. Also probably desperate by now. She was sure he was used to a whole lot more activity.

"I guess nobody warned you that I forget time when I work," she said to Flash as she bent to connect his leash. "Sorry about that, boy." She ruffled his fur and scratched between his ears, but there was no mistaking his eagerness. He moved from paw to paw as if he could barely contain his excitement.

Maybe she should set an alarm to remind her that she needed to make dog time now. She stuffed a plastic bag in her pocket for cleaning up after him.

"Ready?" she asked. Stupid question. The dog was overready. "Flash, heel."

They stepped out the front door together in time to see Cadell pull into her driveway. Once again the official vehicle and the uniform. Dory had never been keen on uniforms, but this guy…well, he filled that khaki uniform exceptionally well.

She waved, and he waved back as he climbed out. "Going somewhere?" he called.

"Flash and I are taking a walk."

"I'll bring Dasher along, too, if you don't mind some company."

Dory didn't even hesitate. For once she was glad of company. The world around her seemed to be growing more threatening by the day, and no amount of internal argument could change the feeling. George was on the streets again. George blamed her for his conviction. She'd heard that clear enough, even though she hadn't testified and had still been in a state of utter shock. "Great. You can tell me if I'm doing it right."

They reached the corner without either of them speaking. Dasher and Flash were completely well behaved, waiting patiently to learn which direction they were supposed to take.

"Any preference about where you want to walk?" Cadell asked.

"Honestly, I've been out jogging nearly every day, but I'm totally unaware of my surroundings. My head is on my projects, and everything else goes away when I run."

Cadell hesitated, then said, "Right now that's not wise, Dory. Yes, you'll have Flash with you, but you need to be aware of your surroundings. Not to mention learning your way around."

She flushed faintly, knowing he was right. Scared as she was of her brother, she couldn't afford to be off in her own world when she was outside. But running cut her free, let her mind wander in ways that could be extremely useful and creative.

She frowned down at the pavement, trying to figure

out how to balance this. Just how afraid was she of George? Afraid enough to pay attention? To relinquish some of her best thinking time?

She lifted her head and looked around the quiet neighborhood. It seemed so benign, her fears so out of place. Yet the neighborhood she had lived in as a child hadn't been much different. Quiet. Benign. And then a monster had emerged in her own house.

"Okay," she said finally. "You're right. I don't like it, but you're absolutely right."

"You don't have to be hyperalert," he said. "You *will* have Flash keeping an eye out. But you at least have to know where you are and develop a sense for when something isn't right. For your own peace of mind, really."

He had a point. She'd skipped jogging yesterday because of George, all the while telling herself how ridiculous she was being. Even if George knew where she was—highly doubtful—it would take him at least some time to get here.

She turned to the right, and they resumed walking. Soon she admitted something that was hard to say out loud. "I think I've endowed my brother with some of the qualities of a supervillain."

"How so?"

"Oh, you know. Finding me. Getting here in an instant, walking through walls… I don't know, exactly. Even if he knew I was here, it would take time for him to arrive. Yet yesterday I skipped my run."

"I'm sorry you skipped your run. But I understand the rest."

She glanced up at him. "How could you possibly understand that kind of insanity?"

"Because I've seen what a truly horrible experience can do to the human mind and heart. The impossible has become possible. Why not all the rest, as well? That's not insanity."

"Maybe not." She couldn't believe she had just revealed that to him. But Cadell seemed like an honestly nice guy, and he'd been understanding of her fears from the outset. Maybe she needed more than one person to talk to. Betty had heard most of it more than once. Maybe all she wanted was a fresh perspective.

"So," he said two blocks later, during which she had tried to pay attention to everything around her, "do you think you might do me a favor?"

Everything inside her tensed. That would depend, she thought, although she stopped herself from saying it out loud. Heavens, the man had given her a beautiful guard dog. She owed him…if she was capable of providing what he wanted.

"What's that?" she asked cautiously.

"One of my friends—also a deputy, by the way—has a five-year-old stepdaughter, almost six. Her dad was a cop who was killed. Anyway, he says she's lately become determined to get a police dog. Neither of us is sure why or what she really wants. So…could I bring her over to see Flash? He hasn't got the kind of training that would make her parents nervous, but he might be exactly what she needs. I don't know. How could I?" He laughed quietly. "I'm not sure where this demand is coming from, but she's adamant. Not a puppy, but a police dog."

Dory felt torn. A little girl who'd lost her dad. She identified with that. But she didn't want to sink social roots in this town. She didn't want to socialize at all. Life was so much clearer when she kept to herself and simply worked. Trust never became an issue.

But a little girl? One not so very different than Dory herself had been once. Some string in her heart began to knit a connection of some kind, like it or not.

"All right," she said. She was sure she didn't sound enthusiastic.

"If it's too much trouble…"

She whirled then. Flash stopped walking and came to stand right beside her, but she hardly noticed. "It's not a matter of trouble. It's a matter of me. I'd rather be a hermit, if you haven't heard. Bring the child over. At least I can trust *her.*"

She resumed her walk with Flash, leaving Cadell and Dasher behind. Well, that was a lunatic sort of thing to have said, she thought irritably. People around here were evidently going to insist on pushing into her life. She needed that to stop.

But then she remembered the gift of the dog trotting beside her and felt like an absolute ingrate. A sleaze. Couldn't she at least put a pleasant veneer over her scarred personality?

Abruptly she halted and pivoted on one foot. Cadell was right there behind her, his face revealing nothing.

"I'm sorry," she said.

"You're under a lot of stress," he replied. "I guess I'm adding to it."

Aw, heck, she thought as they resumed their walk. Now she was making *him* feel like a problem when all he had done was be incredibly kind and understanding. Flash scooted over onto some grass to do his business, and she pulled the plastic bag out of her pocket, picking up the mess, then knotting off the bag.

"You're not adding to anything," she said after a bit. "You've been great to me. The problems are all my own. I'm not usually like this, but…"

"Well, you've moved, your brother is out of prison, you're having problems with that… I'd say that's not usual by any means."

"I don't deserve excuses. I need to learn to handle all this. It's the way life is, now."

And this version of life evidently didn't include her hiding out with her computers and her projects except when she had to emerge to buy groceries. Nope. Now there was Betty nearby, and Cadell, who seemed determined to keep an eye on her, and some little girl who'd lost her daddy.

The idea of the little girl wormed past her defenses, and she felt an ache in her heart. Their stories might be different, but she understood the loss that child must feel, and for the girl it was relatively recent.

"What's your friend's daughter's name?"

"Krystal. Everyone calls her Krys."

"How long ago did she lose her father?"

"Two years now. About anyway."

"How sad." Dory sighed. "Sorry for my outburst. By all means, bring her over to meet Flash. Just call and let me know first."

CADELL SPENT A little time in the backyard with Dory and Flash, refreshing him, but Dory didn't show her usual joy in the exercise. She looked pensive, and he hoped he wasn't responsible for that.

So she wanted to be a hermit. Well, some people were built that way. Completely introverted. The thing was, Dory didn't act introverted. Avoidance was something else altogether. And he gathered from what Betty said that she worked with a team online, chatting with them around the clock.

Now that might not be face time, but it was still a group of relationships she'd built. Did she feel safer because of the distance? Because if there was one thing he'd noted, it was that people could become very close online and could be seriously hurt by people they never set eyes on.

So Dory's fortress might not be as safe as she believed.

But he shoved that aside, thinking of her fears about her brother and how they must be pushing her right now. She'd come here to hide out, and by now she might very much want a hole to disappear into.

Instead he was bringing some new people into her life, one of them a little girl he was sure wouldn't allow her to remain detached. He sensed that Dory was identifying with Krys already.

Now he had to wonder if he'd made a huge mistake by trying to help a friend. But the simple fact was he didn't want Krys to become attached to one of his nearly trained police dogs. They were already assigned. Which left Flash as an example of the dog he could train for her. Even as young as Krys was, she would certainly understand that Flash was Dory's dog, something not as easy to explain at his kennels, where he had a number of dogs and worked individually with their handlers most of the time. Out there it might not be clear that a dog wasn't adoptable.

So that left Dory. And maybe a bit of him trying to get in deeper than he should. He had this little niggle that Krys might be able to pierce Dory's barriers in a way no one else could.

He didn't bother asking why he should care. He just did. Which, he reminded himself, ought to be a huge warning. Klaxons ought to be going off in his head. Time to turn around and walk away.

But he didn't. He was, however, disappointed when she said all too soon, "I've got to get back to work. I have a team waiting on me. They know I went out with the dog, but they're probably wondering if I got kidnapped."

He managed a faint smile. "Do they know about your brother?"

Her face closed instantly. "No."

She headed toward her house, leaving him to find his way out of the fenced backyard. "I'll call before I bring Krys over," he said.

She barely glanced back. "Thanks. Thanks for everything, Cadell."

Thanks for what? he wondered as he let himself and Dasher out the gate and walked to his car. He hadn't done anything. Well, except for giving her a dog she desperately needed.

Shaking his head a little as he put Dasher in the backseat, he wondered at himself. He'd probably way overstepped himself by asking her to let Krys come over. Because it wouldn't just be Krys, and she knew it. It would be Krys and at least one parent.

People she evidently didn't care to meet. Interrupting the life she'd worked long and hard to build for herself.

He snorted at his own folly as he backed out of her driveway. He was acting like a stupid moth, coming back to the flame again and again. But she wasn't a flame. The sight of her might ignite his own fires, but he'd seen enough to know that Dory might singe him with cold. Bitter cold.

DORY SLIPPED BACK into her chair at her desk and soon forgot everything else as she dived into working on her part of the animation they were creating, and chatting with the other members of her team. Mostly they talked business, tools, ways to solve problems and new ideas. Once in a while they became more personal, but she hid herself well. She doubted any of them guessed that D. K. Lake was a woman. Given the harassment of women online, she wanted to keep it that way. Not that any of her colleagues would dump on her, but if word got out that one of Major Animation's creative team was a woman? No, thanks.

After a couple of hours, concentration escaped her and she realized that her thoughts were drifting to other things. God, she been nearly rude to Cadell, if not outright rude.

No, she wasn't thrilled about meeting this little girl, because caring was such a dangerous thing. But a five-year-old? Yeah, she'd have to meet at least one of the parents, but that didn't have to go beyond a half hour or so. The kid wanted a dog. Cadell had thought one trained like Flash, rather than his other dogs, would be best.

Would it kill her to be helpful? Being helpful didn't mean she had to become involved.

Except for Betty, only her godparents had gotten inside the walls erected by one horrific night in her family kitchen. Of course she knew people. She'd made friends all the way through high school and college. But she'd never let those people close. They never met the real Dory Lake, because she never let them. She skimmed the surface with them while holding herself apart.

She'd had enough therapy to know exactly what she was doing, and she had absolutely no desire to change that about herself. That shell she kept around her innermost being was all that protected her. She'd learned that the hard way.

As Flash rested his head on her thigh, and she looked down at him, she realized her wall might have been penetrated. Just a little bit.

Sighing, she patted the dog and returned to work.

Chapter Five

More than a week later, on a Saturday morning, Cadell joined Dan and little Krystal at Dory's house. Last night he'd checked up on George Lake and had found some disturbing news. He didn't know whether to share it or not, but this morning he was determined to let no shadow hover over Krys's meeting with Flash and her desire for a police dog. Maybe later, he'd tell Dory what he'd learned.

She greeted both him and Dan pleasantly at the door, but he noticed circles under her eyes. She wore a burgundy sweatshirt labeled Heidelberg, as if she were chilled on this summer morning, and jeans. Her feet were covered with socks. Beside her, alert, stood Flash, his head cocked inquiringly.

"Come on in," she said, swinging the door wide. "I was just about to put my shoes on."

Once inside her small foyer, introductions were made. She shook hands with Dan, giving him a pleasant smile, then squatted down until she was at eye level with Krys. "I heard about you, Krys. So you want a police dog?"

Krys nodded quickly. "Dan says you have one. Is that him?"

"That's Flash. He's beautiful, isn't he?"

"He's big," came the response. "Can I touch him?"

"Sure. Flash, sit. Shake." That was her own addition to Flash's repertoire, surprisingly easy to teach to this very bright dog. Flash obediently sat and extended his right front paw.

Krys giggled and reached for it. "I like him!"

Flash apparently liked her, too. If dogs could grin, he was grinning now.

"But is he a *real* police dog?" Krys asked. Apparently, she wasn't about to be snowed. Cadell caught the smile on Dory's face as she stood up. She looked at him.

"I trained him," said Cadell. "He's a good guard."

Krys looked up at him. "No biting?"

"No biting." Not exactly true but true enough. "He only bites if you tell him to."

"Mommy says I can't have a dog that bites."

Cadell looked at Dan. Dan half shrugged, then said, "I don't think she meant a dog that wouldn't bite a bad man. Does that worry you, Krys?"

"Not if it's only bad men." Her face grew serious. "There are bad men. One killed my daddy. I wish he had a dog."

Three adults exchanged looks, but as soon as the cloud appeared, it blew away, and Krys asked, "Can I play with him, too?"

"Of course you can," Dan said. He looked at Dory and Cadell. Dory smiled and waved toward the back door. "You guys take him out. I need to finish up something."

BUT INSTEAD OF returning to her computers, Dory wound up standing at the back window of her bedroom, watching the two men and the little girl play with Flash.

God, Krys tugged at her heart. Another child's life forever scarred by someone murderous. She could easily imagine some of what that little girl was living with.

The window was open a few inches to let the summery breeze in, and she heard some of the conversation.

"Flash won't let you tell him what to do," Cadell was explaining. "He only listens to me and Dory. So your dog would only listen to you and your parents, okay? That's part of what makes a police dog different."

So Cadell was going to give that little girl a version of Flash. Dory wondered if the child was haunted by nightmares, or by fears she didn't know how to express.

None of her business, she told herself. Not a thing she could do about it. Returning to her office, she buried her head in her work. Work was her salvation. Creating artificial worlds made her happy.

Little enough else did.

A HALF HOUR LATER, she heard Krys's piping voice go out the front door and assumed she was once again alone. She wished she knew how to reach out better, especially to that little girl. Everything inside her seemed to freeze up, though, leaving her basically useless. God, it would be easy to hate herself.

She heard Flash trotting toward her, and soon his head rested on her thigh. She reached out automatically to scratch his neck while she watched her latest animation unfold on her screen.

Water was rushing into the ground floor of a building, sweeping furniture and other debris before it. As she watched, she was keeping an eye out for ways to improve it.

"That's cool," said a voice behind her.

She nearly jumped out of her skin. Whirling around, she saw Cadell standing in the doorway of her office. Her heart had nearly climbed into her throat, making it impossible for her to speak.

"Very cool," he repeated. "Did you make that?"

She gave a stiff nod.

"I'm impressed. Sorry I startled you—I thought you heard me heading this way. I wanted to thank you for letting Dan and Krys see Flash."

"No problem," she mumbled, waiting for her heartbeat to slow. "Krys can come again, if she wants."

"That's generous of you. I could tell you were uneasy about it. And the way you looked at Krys… At least she didn't see anything, Dory. She was at home in bed when her father was killed."

"Does it matter?" she asked stiffly.

"Sorry?"

It was as if a wrench turned inside her, loosening a huge bolt. Before she knew what she was going to do, she started talking.

"There was this little girl," she said, looking down at her lap. Flash had settled at her feet. "She was just seven years old. She thought her big brother was the best person in the whole world. She worshipped him."

Glancing up, she saw Cadell nodding, his expression utterly grave.

"Her big brother used to play games with her," she continued. "Read her stories. Carry her around on his shoulders. He made her laugh a lot. Their parents were strict, but he made it seem not so bad. Sometimes he said he'd done something when the little girl had really done it so she didn't get punished. And when the little girl couldn't sleep at night because of the fighting, he sometimes came into her room in the dark and told her stories. Safe stories. Stories without people arguing."

"I'm listening," Cadell said quietly.

"Their parents didn't fight a lot. It wasn't often. But then they started fighting with her big brother, and the little girl was bothered. She knew her big brother was staying out too late, and that her parents thought he was doing things he shouldn't, but she thought her big brother was a good guy."

She drew a shaky breath. "She loved her big brother. Until one night. The fighting was loud, bad, scary. They were fighting with her brother. She knew she wasn't supposed to go downstairs, but she was worried about him. So she crept down the stairs and…" Her voice broke. She panted the last words, struggling for the breath to get them out. "She discovered her brother had turned into a monster."

CADELL DIDN'T MOVE for long moments. His chest felt as if steel bands had wrapped around it and were tightening with every breath. For the first time in his life, he absolutely did not know what to do.

Touching her, even to offer comfort, might send her into flight. This was the woman who wanted to be a hermit. Part of him was amazed that she'd told him her story in such an intimate way. Another part of him was alarmed that she was so vulnerable now—a wrong word or movement could lock her down forever.

Something about Krys had drawn this out of Dory, because he was sure he'd done nothing to make it possible for her to drop her guard this way. To open up. Hesitantly, he finally said, "What about Krys?"

At that she seemed to snap into focus and looked at him. Whatever emotions had been rising out of her depths suddenly backed off—swallowed, he thought, by her cultured distance. "Krys? So what if she didn't see anything bad? She went to bed one night and woke up in the morning to learn that her dad was never coming home again. That's hard to deal with."

"I'm sure." He took a tentative step toward her, wishing the tension would leave her face. "So you think the dog will help her?"

"Flash helps *me*."

Well, that sure as hell made him feel good. Finally he reached her and squatted right in front of her chair. The news he'd learned that morning was going to have to wait.

"Can you get away?" he asked.

"Get away?"

"Out of here for a while. For a drive, a walk, whatever."

Perplexity awoke on her face, dispelling some of the tension. "You're in uniform. Don't you have to work?"

"I need to stop by the ranger station for a few minutes. They want some K-9s, too, but it won't take long to sort out. You might enjoy meeting Desi Jenks. She's a pistol. Anyway, can you take some time?"

He watched her hesitate, turning her head to the loop of flooding waters that was repeating on her monitor, almost like she wanted to dive into it. Then he watched a shudder pass through her, as if she were releasing tension. "Okay," she said finally. "I guess I do need to get out for a little while. It'd do me some good. Give me a minute to let my team know I'll be back later."

"What?" he said lightly. "You mean you don't carry them with you on a cell phone?"

At that her demeanor changed entirely, and she smiled faintly. "I've noticed there are a few dead zones around this town."

"We all have that problem. It's getting better but not perfect." He straightened and turned toward her door. "I'll be out front, but I need to get to Desi over her lunch hour." He glanced at his watch. "Which is very soon."

"Okay," she said briskly, once again all business. She turned to her computer, and he watched words popping up on one of the screens not displaying the flood or grids of some kind. "How long should we be?"

"Not long for Desi, probably, but if you want to see a little of the area, give us a couple of hours."

"Okay." She tapped away, chuckled quietly and then faced him again. "Let me get my shoes. Is Flash coming?"

"I hope you don't consider going anywhere without Flash."

"The supermarket might object," she said lightly.

"Then I'll get him a vest. Get your shoes."

DORY FELT ODD, and she acknowledged it as she went to get her jogging shoes. First that unexpected dump about what had happened to her as a child. She wasn't sure what had brought that on, but she had a feeling it very much had to do with Krys. Identification. A need to make it clear to at least one person that losing a parent left wounds behind, no matter whether you saw any part of it.

But she'd never told her story quite that way to anyone. She also hadn't finished it. She wondered if she should. She gave Cadell marks for not reacting as if there was anything he could do. Her experience was in the past, beyond changing, beyond reaching. Long ago she'd grown tired of those who upon hearing about her past wanted to make it better with a hug or trite phrases. She understood everyone had meant well, but it had all been useless. Her soul had been twisted and hammered into a different shape by what she had seen, and nothing was ever going to wrench it back into shape.

At last she left the house, locking it up behind her although she'd once asked Betty why she never locked her house.

Betty had laughed. "Around here? Nobody does."

But not everyone had the kind of expensive computer equipment Dory used. Hers might look just slightly larger than usual towers, but she had several four-thousand-dollar graphics cards in there, not to mention all the add-ons. If she had to replace much of that stuff—never mind her work—she could easily spend twenty thousand dollars or more. So she locked the door and kept the curtains closed all the time to conceal what was inside. Betty might say theft was rare around here, but why hang the temptation out for all to see?

She and Flash climbed into the car with Cadell. Dasher was in the backseat and woofed a greeting. Flash answered.

Dory felt relieved when her sense of humor began to awaken. "They're like best buddies."

"They'll probably have a great conversation with their noses back there. By the time we get to the station, they'll know all about what each has been doing since their last meeting."

Dory smiled, thinking it was very likely possible. "So we're going to meet a ranger?"

"Well, not a ranger, per se. She's the local senior game warden, otherwise known as a redshirt."

"Why redshirt? Or is that obvious?"

He laughed. "Obvious. They all wear red shirts.

Mostly with jeans, boots and cowboy hats, although ball caps are creeping in. Very laid-back approach to uniforms."

She thought it would seem that way to him. His khakis were pressed and even had military creases in the shirt. "Well, with shirts that distinctive, they probably don't have to worry about the rest."

"Nope. They're pretty readily identified."

"I've never met a game warden before."

"You'll like Desi. No nonsense and damn good at what she does. She broke up a ring of unlicensed outfitters last fall. Pretty risky business. But then, her job has its own set of risks. I'm not the one heading out into the woods during hunting season when everyone is armed."

That drew a laugh from her. It felt good to be out, she realized. Sunshine, warm air blowing through the window. She spent too much time in her cave. Seasons could go by almost unnoticed. She averted her head, looking out the window at the small houses they passed, then the open areas. The drive to the station wasn't long, but long enough for her to start wondering if she was in love with her work or if she was hiding in it.

The question made her uncomfortable, and she shoved it aside. George was out of prison. Soul-searching was going to have to wait until she was sure he wanted nothing to do with her.

No reason he should. The words had become almost

a mantra inside her head: *No reason George should want to find her.*

Now all she needed to do was believe it.

GEORGE FOUND HIS sister in remarkably short order. Yeah, it took a few days, but she was a presence on the web because of her design work, no matter how hard she tried to hide behind her initials. Besides, he'd found out about her job years ago.

As for the money he needed…well, that was easy enough to pick up. No rotten job necessary. He'd sweet-talked a woman in her fifties, giving her a sob story that made her invite him to stay with her. It wasn't long before she'd given him all the money he needed, and he was quite sure she'd be too ashamed to tell the cops what had happened.

So he was able to vanish from the halfway house. He told them he'd found a job in another town. None of their concern, since he was a free man and the halfway house was only supposed to be temporary.

He hung around for another week, treating the woman like a queen, feeling sickened every time he made her titter like a girl. At her age. Really.

After that he left for a "job interview" and never went back. Even if she decided to call the cops, she didn't know his real name, she'd never taken a photo of him and he'd been very careful about what he touched…except her. Wiping up after himself had been nearly automatic.

Then he discovered he hadn't found Dory at all. Her

old address had been abandoned a few weeks ago, and her neighbors hardly knew her. No one could say where she'd gone. From the looks on most of the faces of the people he talked to, he gathered they hardly cared about her disappearance and that they really didn't have any idea where she was now.

He cussed and spent some time at the local library using their computers. She had to have left a trail of some kind. She was still working. The only thing was, he'd learned from hard experience that her company didn't release detailed information about the whereabouts of the people who worked for it. The most they gave on their lead designers was a geographic region. Over the phone it became apparent they didn't answer questions about one of their team and they'd never met her. They thought she was a guy.

That amused him a bit. So she was living a pretense. Gutless.

Sighing, needing to put more miles between him and the woman he'd just conned—he couldn't be *positive* she'd be too embarrassed to report him—he left the library and headed down the road.

He'd find her. He knew enough about her from keeping tabs over the years to know her head would poke up eventually. Once she reappeared in one of the chat rooms she had used in the past, he'd be able to find her. Amazing how many details those social sites kept on people even after a decade or more.

When he was in prison, he'd watched plenty of his fellow inmates go to those same rooms because they wanted company. Mostly they wanted some girl to get sweet on them.

He'd avoided all of that. Leaving online traces could be a big mistake. Anyway, as long as he kept moving now and created different email addresses or log-ins at each new location, nobody would be able to track *him*.

But Dory… Dory might be smart about some things, but she probably thought she was safe behind the wall of her company and her alias. No reason for her to imagine, either, that George could find her online. After all, he'd been in prison, and she probably had absolutely no idea just how much you could learn about computers and the internet in prison.

He savored the fact that she probably thought she was perfectly safe where she was now.

She was in for a shock.

DORY FORGOT HER fears for a little while as she met Desi Jenks, a lovely woman with a nimbus of dark curls and a very strong personality. She was clearly in charge, at least as involved her job, and both crisp and clear about what she hoped for in a couple of dogs from Cadell.

"Basically police dogs," she told him. "We'll probably be using them mostly for search and rescue, but I also need them to be able to find shells and bullets so we can triangulate a scene, sniff for drugs…" She paused and laughed. "You know all of this, don't you,

Cadell? What I want isn't so very different from the dogs you train for the sheriff."

"Not really, no," he answered with a smile. "You might make a few additional demands. We'll have to see as we work through it. Will you have vests for them?"

"Orange," she answered properly. "Already on their way."

"At night, hook some glow sticks to them, okay?"

She nodded. "I don't want them mistaken for game, either. You can count on it."

"How many are you thinking?"

"Two for now. Any more and I'll bust my budget."

Cadell's eyes crinkled at the corners. "We'll see what we can do about that."

Then Desi turned to Dory, who was standing silently to the side. "So you're a graphics designer? What kind, exactly?"

"I make animations for films and ads."

Desi's eyes widened. "You mean like that stuff I see in the movies?"

"Some of it. The bigger animation studios do the work on the major films, but we get some thrown our way, and we work on independent productions."

"If I ever find time to get away from here, would you show me something?"

Dory hesitated almost imperceptibly. "Sure."

"Not that I have much free time," Desi said drily.

"Kell and I are still trying to find time to get married and fit in a honeymoon."

"Elope," Cadell suggested. "Call in sick and run away."

Desi laughed loudly. "Sure. As it is we hardly see each other."

Such normal concerns, Dory thought, watching the two of them laugh and chat easily. Maybe hiding in her work all the time was depriving her of something.

But to be that relaxed with other people…it would require more trust than she seemed capable of giving. No, she was better off staying within the world she had created for herself. Just because Betty had turned out to be special didn't mean anyone else would.

"So what breed of dogs do you want?" Cadell asked Desi a few minutes later.

"Whatever works. I'm not particular, and I wouldn't usually need my dogs to be frightening. Most of the time I need them to track. Whatever you can give me that will be willing to traipse through the woods."

Cadell nodded. "I got it. I'll call next week and tell you what kind of selection I can come up with. When I've got a few, you can come out and see what you think."

Cadell seemed lost in thought as they drove away with the dogs in the seat behind them. "I guess I need to let those two take a walk," he said eventually.

"Probably."

He looked over at her. "You okay, Dory?"

"I'm fine. Why?"

He paused. "Well, you said you wanted to be a hermit, and I've been dragging people into your life all day. Not very considerate of me."

"You asked first," she answered. Yeah, it was fatiguing when she wasn't used to being around new people, but she could have said no. However, she wouldn't have missed meeting Krys for anything. That little girl had something special about her and Dory wished she'd been able to escape her own internal frost to spend more time with her. And Desi was nice enough and hadn't pressed Dory in any way that made her uncomfortable.

"I know I asked. I'm just wondering if you felt you couldn't say no."

She was oddly touched by his concern. Most people wouldn't even have thought of that.

They stopped somewhere along a dirt road on a turnout near what appeared to be a stock gate, and Cadell let both dogs off leash to race around and work off energy.

He had a lot of confidence in them, Dory realized. More than she had in Flash. She never walked out the front door with him unless he was leashed.

The dogs were clearly in heaven. Cut loose with no orders to follow, they raced through the grasses like the waves of a sea.

"I know some guys who are going to need a bath when we get home," Cadell remarked. All of a sudden, he barked, "Flash! Dasher! No digging."

Whether they knew that particular command, both dogs immediately raised their heads and stopped working at the ground.

"Come," he said.

With tongues lolling happily, both of them came trotting back. Cadell went to the rear of his SUV and lifted up the tailgate, pulling out a gallon bottle of water and a large metal dog bowl. He set it down while the dogs sat and waited politely. When he'd filled it with water, he said, "Go ahead, guys."

They didn't need further permission. Dory felt another bubble of amusement. "These fellows understand a whole lot more than you told me."

He smiled, still holding the plastic bottle while he waited to see if the dogs wanted more. "There's some disagreement about how much verbal language dogs understand. Some say about hundred words, some say closer to six hundred. They're also very acutely aware of other signals. Think about it, Dory. They talk to each other with sounds, postures, tails, ears…but clearly they understand some verbal commands, so they must have language centers. Given that, they probably understand a whole lot more than we think."

"I'm seeing that right now."

"Maybe." He laughed. "Or maybe you're seeing the fact that we've done this before and they know the drill."

She nodded, watching the dogs splash water everywhere with their tongues. "That would make it hard to figure out."

"Very. But one thing I'm sure of—they're a lot smarter than we give them credit for."

When they were back in the truck, Cadell said, "Let's take them to my place to clean them up. I've got a doggy shower, a whole lot easier than you trying to deal with it in a bathtub. Although I'm sure you could."

She twisted and looked back at two very happy dogs, now flopped on the backseat. "I'm more concerned about the burs than the mud."

"Burs are always fun. And I'll show you how to check them for ticks."

Ticks? Oh, man, she hadn't even thought of that. The notion made her squeamish. "Do I have to?" she asked finally.

That made Cadell laugh. "Well, if you want I can come over and do a tick check every day."

In an instant she realized that she wouldn't at all mind him dropping by every day. Something else to worry about? Because she found it almost impossible to build real connections with other people. The last thing she wanted to do was make Cadell feel bad when he'd been so good to her.

She squared her shoulders and told herself that she *would* learn how to deal with the ticks. She hoped.

"Let's go by my place," he said. "I'll wash the boys up, we can grab a small bite and then I'll take you home."

"Thanks." Then with effort, "How are the ostriches doing?"

"As usual. They're worth a lot of money, as Betty

keeps saying, but I can't sell them. Some inheritance, huh? They hate me, they're expensive to maintain and they drive me nuts. I wish my dad had given me some clue as to what he was thinking when he got them. But none of his friends seem to know, either."

"That's strange."

He shrugged. "My dad was an interesting guy. He would get big ideas of one kind or another, then nothing would happen. Like the time he traded a shortwave radio for a telescope mirror. Admittedly he didn't use the radio, but he never used the mirror, either. It's still sitting on his workbench."

After a minute he said, "I wonder if I could trade two ostriches for a couple of horses."

A giggle bubbled out of Dory. "The horses might be friendlier."

"Oh, there's no question of that."

They drove through miles of open rangeland on the way to Cadell's ranch. The land rolled gently, hinting at the mountains that rose to one side like a huge, distant wall. Herds of deer or antelope grazed alongside cattle, and she wondered if the ranchers minded.

But slowly, ever so slowly, the bigness of the space around her planted uneasiness inside her. Out here there was no place to hide. You could run forever and still be visible.

Why was she having these thoughts? George. But George had no idea where she was. She tried to shake the creeping sense of unease but was failing miserably. She needed the protection of small spaces, walls, locked doors and windows. She needed to keep the bogeyman out.

That drew her up short. The bogeyman? Her brother was no bogeyman. He was a murderer, yes, but for all that he was human. She had no idea why he'd killed their parents, whether it had been born of a rage that caused him to lose control or if he was a seriously broken man. But either way, he wasn't some mythical beast. Just a man.

But the uneasiness wouldn't leave her. The skin on the back of her neck crawled, although there was no reason for it. She had enough scars, she scolded herself. Was she going to live in terror for the rest of her life because George was out of prison? That didn't impress her as a great way to spend the next forty or fifty years.

She was relieved when they reached Cadell's ranch. He had buildings she could run into. Lots of dogs that were being trained to be protective. And two ostriches that would probably love to peck George's eyes out.

That last thought at last made her laugh as tension seeped away.

"What?" asked Cadell.

"I was imagining your ostriches pecking out George's eyes."

As he switched off the engine and set the brake, he gave her one of those smiles that crinkled the corners of his eyes. "Feeling bloodthirsty?" he asked lightly.

"I guess. Better than feeling afraid."

His expression sobered instantly, but he didn't reply directly. "You can go inside if you want and hunt through my fridge for something. The thing is full of leftovers, and there are some soft drinks. I'll just take the dogs to the shower."

"You were going to show me how to check for ticks."

"Actually not difficult if you pet your dog a lot. But yeah, come along and I'll show you."

He *did* have a doggy shower, a concrete room with a sprayer attached to a long hose. Both dogs appeared to be used to the drill and didn't put up a fuss. One by one they stepped in to be shampooed and rinsed. Cadell ran his hands over them as he washed and told her she needed to pay attention to any little bump.

Even as he spoke, a tick fell off Dasher and disappeared down the drain. "Not attached yet," he remarked.

"What do I do if they've already burrowed in?"

"I like nail polish."

Her voice broke on a surprised laugh. "You like what?"

"Nail polish. Once their heads are buried, they have to breathe out the back end. You cover that with polish, and they'll back out real fast. I also don't want to chance leaving a head embedded by pulling on them. It could get infected. So a dab of nail polish, they back out, I grab with tweezers and dump them down the nearest drain or toilet."

"Seems like a good idea to me. I've heard of using something hot."

"Well, you can do that, too. But I figure why risk burning the dogs? Just be careful not to get the polish all over their coats. It only takes the thinnest smear to conquer a tick."

When he finished rinsing Dasher, he said, "Stand back."

She soon learned why. The dog began to shake out his coat, and water flew everywhere. Then he dashed out of the shower and up and down the run, shaking himself again at every kennel he passed.

"He's sharing the shower," Cadell remarked. "Flash, get in."

Dory would have almost sworn that Flash sighed, but he did as he was told, standing perfectly still. This time Cadell handed her the shampoo and spray. "He needs to know you can do this, too."

Well, she couldn't argue with that, and anyway, it was better than thinking about creepy things that could watch her across the open miles out there. Not for the first time she wondered if she were losing her mind.

Flash proved mercifully tick-free, and he seemed to like the warm water rinse the best of all. Then she got to watch him shake out and run up and down as if full of excitement.

Cadell spoke. "I've never been able to decide if they do that because they're so glad to be done with the shower, or if they're just happy."

"They look happy to me." And they did. For a few minutes, Dory forgot everything else. Flash did that for her. Even if he never did another thing, he released her inside, if only for a short while.

"I love that dog," she announced.

"I believe the feeling is mutual."

She looked at Cadell then, daring to meet his gaze directly without sliding quickly away. His gaze was warm, inviting, suggesting delights she could barely imagine. Yet he remained a perfect gentleman with her. He was getting past her guard, little by little. Just as Betty had. She tried to tell herself that wasn't a bad thing. A man who'd give her a dog like Flash had to be special. All the hours of training…she'd bet he didn't do that for free very often. Yet, he'd insisted Flash was merely an extension of his job as a lawman.

Um, wow?

An electric shock seemed to zing between them. Something invisible was trying to push her closer to him. Was he magnetic or something?

But then he broke their gaze and turned. "Wanna come inside and rummage through my fridge before I take you back?" He glanced at his watch. "I go on duty in a couple of hours."

The moment broken, she tried to find steady ground in the practical. "After the shower I think you're going to need a fresh uniform."

He looked down at himself and laughed. "What's a little water?"

Yup, in addition to sexual attraction she was learning to like him a whole lot. Sexual attraction she could deal with. She'd sent more than one guy away over the years, because she wasn't going to get that close to anyone.

But liking? That could be even more of a risk. Sex

she could refuse, because she didn't want to be vulnerable and couldn't trust a guy that much. But liking... well, it grew of its own accord, and she had no idea how to prevent it. Nor did she know if she should. She didn't have to let him that far inside.

Although telling him part of her story earlier, reaching back to the little girl who had been terrorized for life by what she'd seen...well, that had involved trust, hadn't it? Trust that he wouldn't minimize it or tell her to get over it. No, he'd accepted her confidence in silence, not judging at all.

Maybe she was more afraid of judgment than trust. After all, her brother had done something inexplicable. Maybe she thought others judged her to be as bad. Or maybe it was herself she couldn't trust.

Hell. It was a mess, and she didn't want to think about it now. She needed to get back to work. Flash made her feel safe. Just leave it all at that.

They passed the ostrich pen on their way to the house. For once the ostriches didn't even look at them. Instead they stared out over the open fields, away from the mountains. Longing to run free?

But as she was about to cross the threshold behind Cadell, something stopped her. She pivoted sharply and looked out over the endless grasslands. The back of her neck prickled. No reason. Nothing out there.

Maybe she was just reacting to the ostriches' behavior. Or to her own fears.

Shrugging, she followed Cadell inside. Leftovers were beginning to sound good.

BEFORE LEAVING ON his patrol, Cadell checked to see if he'd gotten any pings on the whereabouts of George Lake. Nothing. After a bit of internal argument earlier, he'd decided not to tell Dory that her brother had left the halfway house. It was probably meaningless; the guy wasn't required to stay there since he'd finished his sentence. It might only mean he'd gotten a job offer in another town.

Odd, though, that nobody at the house had any idea where he'd gone or why. All they could tell him about George was that he'd spent a lot of time on their computer when he first arrived.

That made Cadell uneasy, but he'd need a warrant to get a cop out there to look at the computer and find out what George had been so interested in. Unfortunately, uneasiness was not a valid reason to get a warrant. He was lucky the people at the halfway house had told him as much as they had.

No one else in town was likely to know anything anyway. Dory had moved from there with her godparents before she reached middle school, so she had no connections in that town at all. After twenty-five years, there probably weren't even many people who remembered those long-ago murders, or would care that George Lake was hanging around town briefly.

Dead end. So it was good he hadn't said anything to Dory about George's whereabouts. All he'd do was make Dory even more anxious, and she was already anxious enough.

Being a cop had made him acutely aware of people's

unspoken reactions. He'd detected her uneasiness in the open spaces. He'd even picked up on the sudden fright that had made her turn around on his doorstep and look out over empty fields.

He wished he could ease her mind, but all he could do was try to pinpoint one man among millions. Not likely unless the guy crossed the law somehow.

Well, if this was all he could do, he'd do it. And he'd keep an eye on her, too, as unobtrusively as possible.

Because he truly didn't think her fears were unfounded. Not with that inheritance hanging out there.

Chapter Six

George didn't especially want to be found—not yet, at least—but he faced a conundrum anyway. Yeah, he'd taken that woman for quite a bit of money he could get by on, but it was difficult to get by anywhere when you didn't have identification.

He'd been told to take his release papers and his prisoner ID to a Social Security office to try to obtain a Social Security card. He wondered if anyone in the prison system had looked lately at how many proofs of identity were required to achieve that. He hadn't had a driver's license in twenty-five years and didn't think anyone would just hand him one. Getting a birth certificate turned into another set of hurdles.

Not that he wanted to put himself back on the map just yet, but although he had the cash to do it, he couldn't even buy a beater of a car without some ID. That meant he'd have to steal one and hope he didn't get stopped on a road somewhere.

In all his dreaming about what he was going to do to Dory and how rich he was going to be once he got his rightful inheritance, he'd never once considered that even though he was outside the gates, he might as well still be inside. Every avenue seemed blocked—except committing crimes.

There was an irony that he was far from appreciating.

It fueled an old rage in him, but that wasn't helping

anything. Not one bit. There was only one crime he wanted to commit, and he sure as hell didn't want to leave a trail of smaller crimes over a wide swath of the country. That would draw as much attention as getting himself a valid ID.

He knew of a guy who made fake IDs, but he wasn't cheap. George hadn't soaked the woman for enough to cover that *and* still be able to travel. Hell, he should have thought all this through better.

But he did have one breakthrough. He noticed a fresh change at the website of the animation business Dory worked for. One of the designers was now listed as living in Conard County, Wyoming. Seemed a stupid thing to put up, but the feeling he got was that the group was trying to make it clear they could work from all over the country. How that was helpful, he had no idea. He knew how it helped him, though. Well, sort of. A county was a big place.

He was sure it was Dory, though. The timing of the change was too close to his release. Evidently she never wanted to see him again, but that was fine by him. Now that he knew where to look, he just had to get there and scope the situation.

Then he spent some time enjoying daydreams. Did she guess he was coming? Did she even remotely understand that he needed her dead or why? How surprised she was going to look when she saw him.

He remembered the kid sister, the one he had read to and played with, but that kid, the one who had loved him, had died the night she'd run screaming from the house before he could clean up, make it look like someone had broken in. It was her fault he'd gone to prison.

He wondered if she remembered that.

DORY ERUPTED ON the conference. All caps got attention, and she was typing them to her cohort.

WHO THE HELL PUT MY WHEREABOUTS ON THE WEBSITE?

We always do.

THE VICINITY OF KANSAS CITY IS A WHOLE LOT DIFFERENT THAN WHAT YOU'VE PUT UP THERE.

But it's a whole county.

IT'S A COUNTY WITH HARDLY ANY PEOPLE!

The team leader stepped in. Do we need to take this to Skype?

Dory drew deep breaths, steadying herself. Did she want her team members to know she was a woman? Did she want them to see her face? How many people might they tell?

No, she typed, forcing herself to be calmer. Please take that information down immediately. My brother's a murderer. He just got out of prison. I don't want him to find me.

Consider it done, the team leader typed back. I just removed it. We didn't know. I'm sorry, D.K.

She refreshed the webpage and saw that Reggie was as good as his word. It was gone already. She just hoped it hadn't been there for long. And why the hell had she even told them where she going? Because she'd had to explain why it would take her so long to get back on the grid? Because at the time it had seemed innocent enough? Because she hadn't been paying attention to what they put on the webpage?

Because in her panic she hadn't been thinking clearly enough. There was no other reason. She'd let slip some information because she'd been too afraid to realize that it might be unsafe to share with her co-workers. Because all she'd been concerned about was getting away from her last known address as Dory Lake.

Brilliant. She wanted to kick her own butt.

A whimper drew her attention, and she looked down. Flash was lying right beside her, but as he stared up at her without lifting his head, she got the distinct impression he was unhappy. He must be picking up on her anxiety.

He needed something to do, she decided, some purpose. She'd given him little enough, and right now she was in no mood to take a walk or a jog. Heck, right now she didn't even want to step out her front door.

Because she couldn't escape the feeling that George might have found out who she worked for. It wasn't exactly the biggest secret on the planet. And if he knew that, what if he'd found that change on the webpage? She had no idea at all how long that change had been up.

God!

She looked into Flash's soulful eyes and took pity on him. He needed something to do, and she needed something from him. "Flash, guard."

At once he was on his feet, tail wagging. Then, as if he understood, he left her side to check out the other rooms in the tiny house. When he returned a short while later, he lay down with his back to her, head erect, ears alert. He was definitely on duty.

That should have made her feel better. After all, she *had* seen what he could do. But a dog as her only protection?

How was she to continue? Bad things could happen no matter what. She knew that indelibly. But nobody could live in the constant expectation that something bad waited around every corner. Her therapist had tried to hammer that home.

But that was also a kind of trust that Dory found difficult to gain. Trust that nothing bad would happen? Yeah, right.

A ping drew her attention back to one of her monitors. It was Reggie on private chat. You dropped out. Everything okay?

Yeah. Just taking some time to cool off.

She was grateful that he let it go. So how's that flood simulation going?

I'll have the roughed-out version ready for you in a few days.

Great. Ping me if you need anything.

Work, she told herself. *Just get to work.* She could bury herself in the intricacies of bringing a writer's idea to vivid full-dimensional life. An endlessly fascinating process, and no matter how much of it she did, there was still more to learn.

She started up the flood sequence again, looking for any points that would give it away as animation. Animations of human beings were nearly impossible to make so real that you couldn't tell it was an animation. But the stuff like this? It could fool just about anyone if she did it right.

She turned her viewing angle around slowly, seeking any hitches in the way the water moved. Just as she thought she might have found a problem, the doorbell rang.

Part of her wanted to ignore it, but then she noticed Flash had risen to his feet and was wagging his tail excitedly. He glanced back over his shoulder as if to say, "Hurry up!"

So it was someone he knew. She could guess who that was. Much as she wasn't eager to admit it, she wanted to see Cadell again. It had been over a week.

Betty had only popped in once. For a hermit, she was starting to feel a bit lonely.

She was right. She opened the door to find Cadell standing there holding a big brown bag, dressed casually in jeans and a black T-shirt. "Hey," he said. "I brought dinner if you have time."

Flash was sitting obediently beside her, but his hindquarters were twitching as if he wanted to jump up on Cadell.

Trying to shake away the fog in her head, she stepped back. "You'd better come in and pet Flash before he decides to jump on you. I guess he's been missing you." Then she remembered her last command to Flash had been to guard. Quickly she squatted down, catching his head in both hands and rubbing him. "It's okay. Playtime."

Happily he danced away, following Cadell into the kitchen. "I guess you've taught him a new command," Cadell remarked as he began to remove foam containers from the bag. "Maude's finest," he added as he put things on her shaky table. "I'm assuming you're a carnivore?"

"Absolutely."

"Thank goodness. If you'd said you were vegan, I'd be looking through here trying to find something you can eat. I'm not even sure the salad would be safe. I think Maude puts blue cheese in it."

She wished she could laugh, when he was trying so hard to be lighthearted, but laughter felt far away.

"I hope I didn't disturb your work."

"No." Truthful as far as it went. Concentration seemed to have escaped her since the shock earlier of finding her whereabouts on the website. She vaguely knew they listed her general vicinity but hadn't really paid it much attention. Why the heck hadn't she thought to tell them not to change it, or just not tell them exactly where she was going?

They were seated across from one another at the table when he spoke again. He pushed a tall coffee her way, then popped open the boxes for her to choose. "I'm not fancy. Just dig into whatever looks good." He passed her plastic utensils.

She should get out some of her few dishes, she thought. Not that she had many. She'd never needed more than one person could use.

But then Cadell rattled her. "What's wrong?" he asked bluntly.

"Wrong?" she repeated. She hadn't said anything.

"It was written all over your face when you opened the door. You had Flash on guard, I could tell. What's going on?"

She forgot the delicious-looking spread in front of her, any possible appetite disappearing. "Probably nothing." God, she hated being always afraid, and most likely afraid of an eventuality that would never happen. How many times did she have to ask herself why in the world George would ever want to find her? Was there something wrong with her?

Cadell surprised her with a sudden change in tack. "Did you testify against your brother?"

She drew a sharp breath, her vision narrowing until she was looking down a long, dark tunnel. All of a sudden she was standing in that street again, screaming, screaming and not really knowing why, just knowing in her child's heart that everything in her world was broken forever.

"Dory? Dory!" A hand gripped her upper arm gently. Cadell's voice reached her through the darkness. "Tell me," he said. A quiet command.

"Red paint," she said. "Red paint." She sagged into him, dimly feeling his arms close around her. It all came back, every bit of it, worse than the nightmares. Then everything went black.

THERE WAS A rickety couch in the front room, and Cadell carried Dory there, settling her on his lap.

What had he said? What had he done? He'd sent this woman into flight deep within herself, so deep it might be worse than a faint. All he'd asked was if she'd testified against her brother. If she had, she might have some real reasons to be afraid. She might not have even considered that her inheritance could be a threat. He'd found during his law enforcement career that most people didn't have naturally suspicious minds. They didn't think like criminals. Those kinds of ideas just didn't occur to them.

He hadn't even told her that her brother had disappeared from the halfway house after only two days. He had every right to move on, and leaving a place like that was understandable, especially if you hooked up with someone who could help you get on your feet. Lots of prisoners had contacts on the outside, some cultivated in prison. How else did they manage? Family, friends, a few agencies…

He felt a shudder pass through Dory. Looking down, he saw her eyes, as blue and deep as a cloudless sky, open. A Botticelli angel.

Only this angel was feeling like no angel. She squirmed, struggling to get off his lap. He refused to let her go. "Easy, Dory. Easy. It's just me."

It was then he saw Flash. Staring at him. His lip slightly curled. Ready to attack to protect her, but unsure because it was Cadell.

"Dory, snap out of it before your dog rips off half my face."

That reached her. Those amazing eyes abruptly focused. She looked up at him, then over at the dog. "Flash, stay." Then back to Cadell. "I don't know what happened, but you'd better let go of me."

Wow, talk about feeling as if he'd been slapped in the face. He released her immediately, ignoring his body's natural response to her wriggling off his lap. "I was worried about you," he muttered. "You all but fell out of your chair."

An eternity passed before she spoke. Flash, at least, settled at her feet, but he kept eyes on Cadell. "I'm sorry," she said finally.

"You don't have to be. I just don't understand what happened. I asked a simple question, then you said something like 'red paint,' and you were gone. Collapsing. Like you'd fainted."

When she didn't speak, he asked, "Do you need some water or something?"

"Water, please. My mouth feels like cotton."

He rose, went to the kitchen and found one of her two glasses in a cupboard beside the sink. He filled it with water and returned, saying lightly, "You could use a few more dishes."

She nodded but didn't look at him. At least she didn't object when he sat beside her. She took the glass and drained it, leaving little droplets of water on her lip that he'd have loved to lick away. Then he caught himself. Damn, was he losing his mind? This was neither the time nor the place, and most likely not the right woman. Besides, having been badly burned once, he wasn't about to volunteer for another round.

"I'm sorry," she said again.

"Dory…" He gave up. She wouldn't even look at him now, and he'd already told her she didn't need to apologize.

"Red paint." She spoke in a voice so tight it sounded as if it were ready to snap. "I never told you. I don't know if I ever even told Betty. But for a time after the…murder, I was blind and couldn't speak except for two words. *Red paint.* I thought all that blood was red paint."

A seven-year-old girl? Of course she would have no other way to explain it. It also gave him a very clear idea of just how much blood she'd seen. Man, he ached for her. For the child who had been exposed to such horror.

"Anyway," she said, her voice a little steadier, "they said it was a conversion disorder. Someone explained it to me years later. I couldn't handle what I'd seen, so I shut down. My vision came back after a couple of months, but for a year I could speak only two words."

"Red paint."

"Exactly." She let go of a long breath. "All of a sudden, when you asked me if I'd testified against George, I was back there. On that street, screaming. I don't know how long I screamed. I vaguely remember the neighbors running up, the cop cars, the lady police officer who took me away. After that, I don't remember much except my godparents taking me home with them. I was terrified because I couldn't see. As for talking... I never really wanted to talk again."

Taking a risk, Cadell reached out and covered her small hand with one of his much bigger ones. He was relieved when she didn't pull away. He felt the faintest of tremors in her hand.

"Anyway," she said eventually, "I have nightmares about that night. They'd almost stopped, but they've come back big-time since I heard George was being released. Why did he get only twenty-five years? I've never understood that."

"Lots of things play into charging and sentencing," he said carefully. "You could talk to our local judge, Wyatt Carter, if you want. I'm sure he could give you an in-depth answer. All I can tell you is from my own experience. First-degree murder is very hard to prove, for one thing. Intent isn't always easy to prove in a courtroom, and that's the only way he would have gotten a life sentence unless there were aggravating circumstances. If you want my guess…"

"Yes, please."

"An argument with your parents. Tension for some time, from what you said. Your brother lost his temper and saw red. A crime of passion, without premeditation. That weighs into the charges a prosecutor thinks she can sell to the jury. It would certainly play into his defense. Basically, I guess what I'm saying is your brother's sentence wasn't unusual given the circumstances and his youth, being only fifteen at the time. I know that doesn't make you feel any better…"

"No, it doesn't," she interrupted. "Not at all. He butchered them, Cadell. *Butchered* them."

He dared to squeeze her hand and was relieved when she turned hers over and wrapped her slender fingers around his.

"So," she asked on a shaky breath, "how likely is he to do something like that again?"

He couldn't answer that truthfully. A quarter century in prison could straighten out a man's head, or twist it more. "I don't know," he admitted.

"No one can know," she said quietly. "No one." Then she switched course. "That dinner you brought is getting ruined and I'm suddenly hungry."

He watched her stand and leave the room, Flash at her side.

Each new thing he learned about Dory filled him with more respect for her. She'd built a life for herself on some very brutal ashes. He knew well enough that kids all over the world had to survive as she'd survived because of war and natural disaster, but that didn't make her any less remarkable.

Before he followed her, he allowed himself to reflect on his marriage, on the woman whose unceasing demands had left them both so unhappy. What a difference. Somehow he didn't think Brenda could have survived half of what Dory had been through, or at least not with as much grace.

"Cadell? Are you coming?"

He rose and went to join the angel who hadn't fully spread her wings for a quarter century.

THE FOOD WASN'T that cold. Neither of them opted to microwave the steak sandwiches.

"I like cold beef," Dory announced. "Cold roast beef sandwiches are at the top of my list."

"Mine, too. Although the way I live, I seldom cook at home, so no roast beef."

"I should make one," she said. "We can share it. The only reason I don't do it more often is that to get a well-cooked roast, you need more than I could ever eat by myself. And I don't like it as much if I freeze it for later."

"Well, that's one job you can expect my help with. Let me buy the roast. You cook, I'll carve."

She laughed, a small one, but enough to ease his

heart a bit. She was looking forward again, at least for now. It wouldn't last forever. In fact he'd probably have to be the one who shattered her hard-won peace.

While they were putting the leftovers away, he said, "You looked upset when I got here. You never said why."

She shook her head a little, drying her hands on a dish towel. "I was furious because my company put my whereabouts on their webpage. They thought it was vague enough. I had to explain that Conard County is underpopulated."

"Wait," he said almost sharply. "Back up. Why do they include anything about where you live?"

"I guess it's felt that since we don't have a central office we might make an advantage out of being scattered all over the country but still working together. Major Animation has three teams like mine. And we *are* scattered all over."

"Okay. I suppose I can get that. Centralized without being located in one place. So how detailed are the locations?" His heart had sped up a bit. He didn't like the way he was feeling right now. Worry had begun to gnaw at him like a hungry rat.

"Well, for example, they used to have me listed as being in the vicinity of Kansas City. There are a lot of people there, and nobody could have found me easily. But I screwed up. I guess I wasn't thinking clearly. Anyway, I told someone on my team where I was moving, and today I saw it on the webpage. Conard County,

Wyoming. They thought listing an entire county was vague enough."

"Not if it's this county," he agreed. "So what then?"

"They took it down. I doubt anyone noticed it."

He wished he was sure of that. "Does it have your full name?"

She shook her head. "I go by D. K. Lake. It's not even my real middle initial."

Good enough, he thought sourly, even with a wrong middle initial. If he'd discovered somehow that she was working for this company, he'd have no trouble finding her now no matter how common the last name Lake was—and it was. "So nobody's thinking about personal security for you guys?" He found that hard to stomach.

"We're just a bunch of graphics designers. Most of the people we deal with are ad companies, indie film-makers…it's not like we're putting our life stories out there." She looked down. "Except today. I raised Cain. I had to tell them about my brother."

He took a step closer. "And you didn't like that."

"Of course I didn't!" She rubbed her arms from shoulder to wrists, one after the other as of trying to push something away. "It's like an invisible stain. My brother is a murderer. Worse, he killed our parents. What does that say about him, about me, about our family?"

Oh, God, he was going to be wishing he had a grad-uate degree in psychology before much longer. Opening and closing his hands, he tried to find something to say, something that might actually comfort her.

The only thing that occurred to him was a question. "Do you really believe that, Dory? Do you think you could ever have done what your brother did?"

Her entire face froze, grew still and motionless. For a few seconds, he feared he'd pushed her back into the horror, but then she shook her head. "No," she said. "I don't think I could have, ever. But who can know that, Cadell? Perfectly ordinary people go over the edge all the time."

"I'm a cop," he reminded her. He nudged her back to one of the chairs at the table and brought her one of those orange soft drinks she seemed to like so much. He unscrewed the cap before he put it on the table.

"So?" she said. "You're a cop. What's that mean?"

"I like this town because it's pretty peaceful most of the time. But I've worked in much bigger towns. What you saw your brother do? I've seen that and a helluva lot more. There's no limit to what human beings are capable of."

She tilted her head, looking up at him. "And that's comforting why?"

"I'm not sure it's comforting. But I can tell you something—there were warning signs in every one of those cases. Something askew. Maybe nobody noticed it in time, but those signs were there. Tensions building. Things being said or hinted at. A withdrawal, maybe. But by the time an investigation was complete, we almost invariably had a profile of someone who'd been sending out warnings like invisible flares for months, maybe years. Very, very few cases erupted out of nowhere, and when they did drugs were often involved."

She nodded slowly. He slid into the other chair across from her. "The thing is," he continued, "the vast majority of people never kill, and even fewer of them kill in the way your brother did. He's in a very small group. There's no reason to even wonder if you could do what he did. To feel like it's a taint of some kind. Your parents weren't murderers, were they? Have *you* ever wanted to do something like that?"

"God, no!" She shuddered as her eyes widened.

"You have no reason to be ashamed because your brother went off the rails. One of the cops I used to work with back in Seattle had a brother who was a con man. You couldn't ask for two more different guys, and they came out of the same genetic stock into the same environment. Ralph hated it, though. He was frustrated, he couldn't talk sense to his brother, and occasionally we'd arrest the guy and put him away for a few years. Ralph took some ribbing, but if ever anyone had an excuse to want to kill someone it was Ralph. His brother was good at preying on people, but as angry as it made Ralph feel, he'd put his brother in handcuffs and bring him in. He never tried to hurt him."

"Wow," she said quietly. "That's awful."

"It sure was for Ralph. He was convinced it was holding him back in his career. I don't know if it was. I mean, the higher you go, the harder it is to move up because there are fewer slots. But Ralph believed the department never quite trusted him. I know all us guys who worked with him trusted him completely."

Deciding he'd said enough for now, and feeling thirsty himself, he helped himself to a soft drink from her fridge, choosing cola.

When he came back to the table and sat, Dory had reached for a paper napkin and was creasing it absently. "I've always felt that something must be wrong with me," she admitted. Then she raised her head and smiled faintly. "Well, obviously there are some things wrong with me by other people's estimation. I'm mostly a hermit, I don't trust people much at all...but I'm talking about something else."

"I know you are."

She compressed her lips and nodded. "When something like that happens so close to you, especially in your own family, maybe you always feel different."

"Maybe." He tilted the bottle to his lips and drank deeply, figuring he'd said as much as he could or should. From what she'd mentioned, he gathered she'd had plenty of therapy. He had no business mucking around with whatever peace she'd managed to make.

"I'm sorry if I'm interrupting your work," he said. It suddenly occurred to him that he'd come over uninvited, meaning only to stay about a half hour, but with what had happened he'd been here much longer.

"Not really," she said. "I put in most of a day before I erupted at my team about the website."

"Well, I'd still better go." He glanced at his watch and realized it was getting late. Flash dozed near Dory, but he'd wake at the slightest sound. She was in good paws, he decided. He also decided not to tell her about George yet.

She'd been through hell tonight, all because of his question.

Dory sighed and went back into her office. He and Flash followed her, and as soon as she sat Dory seemed to be watching her simulation intently, was probably at least halfway back into her work. Time to go. Cadell opened his mouth to say good-night.

But then she spoke, surprising him. "So your wife couldn't handle being married to a cop?"

Astonished, he didn't answer immediately, but then tried for lightness. "Please be sure to include the *ex* part when calling her my wife. And her name was Brenda."

She turned from her screen, her hand still on her mouse, and her eyes danced a bit. In that instant she looked positively edible. "Kinda bitter?"

"That isn't the word I'd use. Not anymore anyway. I was certainly angry, back then. I felt as if she'd been lying to me from the moment we met, although that probably wasn't a fair feeling. She just had no concept of what she was getting into, and once she got there she didn't like it. A longer engagement might have been wise. In that case it probably would have helped." He shrugged. "But you never know. It only lasted two years, but that was plenty for both of us. I'm just glad we didn't have kids, because that would have made it a tragedy."

"It would indeed," she said quietly, her face shadowing. Well, of course. He'd reminded her of what it was like to lose parents.

For a half minute he actually contemplated just keeping his mouth shut around her. Then he realized that walking on eggshells would be unsettling for both of them. He decided to offer her another nugget of truth before he left.

"With Brenda," he said, "I learned something. At the time I just wanted to be with her, and I didn't think about giving her the wrong idea. I switched quite a few of my shifts with my buddies so Brenda and I could have a night out, do something she wanted to do, whatever. So if she expected that to continue, it was my fault and nobody else's."

She nodded slowly, her face smoothing again. Dang, she was beautiful. Hard to believe that so much ugliness resided in her memory and haunted her life.

"So it couldn't continue?" she asked.

"Nope. My buddies were great, but eventually it became a problem. The brass started objecting, I got a few sarcastic comments about why I didn't just tell them when I'd be available to work…"

"Ouch." She winced, then smiled. "That would do it."

"It sure did. So I have to take a measure of responsibility for Brenda's disappointment." It had a taken him a while to face that, but it was a lesson well learned, and one good reason not to tiptoe around Dory. Only honesty could build her trust. If she ever built any real trust in him.

He stirred. "Anyway, I've taken up your entire evening, and that wasn't my intention. I'll be off now."

Something in the way her blue eyes looked at him seemed almost like an appeal. But what kind of appeal? He couldn't imagine what she might want from him. This was a woman who'd told him at least twice that she preferred to be a hermit.

Suddenly, moved by an impulse that even to him seemed to come out of nowhere, he squatted before her, not touching her. "You're beautiful, you know," he murmured. "You remind me of a Botticelli angel."

She blinked, looking uncertain. Enough, he thought. He could kick his behind when he got home. Straightening, he turned toward the door.

"Cadell?"

He half turned. "Yeah?"

"You're a hunk."

Startled, he looked directly at her, then began to laugh. "Imagine the painting that would come out of that." Then he resumed his exit, pausing only to say good-night to Flash.

Dory laughed quietly. The painting that would come out of that? An angel and a cop? Or a cowboy? It was humorous, all right.

But gradually her humor faded. The night had closed in around the house, and she felt it as an almost physical pressure. "Flash, guard."

He obeyed, sitting beside her, alert.

Alone but not alone. Who would have thought she'd be so grateful for a dog? And what had happened just now with Cadell? She'd revealed things to him during her flashback that she was sure she'd never told anyone but her therapist. She could hear her own voice as she told the story of that night in third person, as if she were removed from it, yet still sounding a bit childlike.

He'd handled it well. Why not? He was a cop—he'd probably seen it all. Part of her was surprised that when all that had burst out the triggers of memory had made her turn to him, a near stranger. She didn't *do* that.

She tried to lose herself in work, but her mind refused to cooperate. The door to the past had opened tonight, and she felt it was as fresh as yesterday.

Damn.

Then, turning to her other computer, she brought up an image she had constructed of that terrible night. She didn't know why she had felt compelled to render it with near photo realism, but she had done it a few years ago. There it sat, just as she had seen it as a child.

What good did that do? What earthly use could it have? What part of her mind needed it? Did she think that by looking at it over and over again that she'd become desensitized?

Did she really want to become desensitized to such horrific violence?

No.

But she sat staring at it as if mesmerized. Her brother, they had said later when she could understand such things, had evidently been a drug user. Cocaine could wreck the mind and turn some people violent. Blame it on cocaine?

Hitting a key, she made the image vanish and considered just erasing it. It held no answers for her. There could be no real answer to what had happened that night. No satisfactory explanation for that kind of act.

She heard a ping and turned to see that Reggie, the team leader, had reentered the chat. Looking for her.

D. K. You there?

She hesitated then typed her answer. Yeah.

I'm really sorry about the mess up on the website. I just want to be sure you're okay.

Yeah, she replied. Like she was ever really okay.

The webmaster fixed your location. You're back to where you used to be.

Thanks, Reggie.

No problem. Countable seconds passed before he typed something else. Look, we're all worried about you. You need anything at all, ping me or Skype me. I'm usually within a few feet of this damn machine.

Me, too. Played any good games lately? Anything to get off this subject.

Nothing new, he admitted. I'm still trying to beat the goblin at the gate so I can get to the reward. Damn smart goblin.

Her spirits lifted more as they chatted about the game they sometimes played together, although she wasn't really into spending hours gaming the way some were. The advanced games that might hold her attention involved teaming up, and that made her as uneasy on the computer as it did in real life.

After a few more minutes, she signed off the chat claiming fatigue, but she didn't feel fatigued at all.

She didn't want to go to sleep. She didn't want another nightmare.

Closing her eyes, she thought about Cadell, surprised that she'd told him he was a hunk. Even more surprised that he thought she looked like an angel.

Forget Cadell, she told herself. How could she be sure he wouldn't rip her heart to shreds the way George had? Maybe not with violence, but in some other way.

She sighed, rested her chin in her hand and tried to study her scene. It sat there frozen, waiting for her attention to the misplaced vortex. There were a lot of items she needed to add, all of them listed in a file she'd received from Reggie. Every one of them had to be constructed. They weren't, unfortunately, items that the team had in its library from previous builds.

De novo. From scratch. She usually loved the challenge. Tonight she wasn't loving much of anything.

Flash stood, stretched and shook himself out before

resuming his position at her side. Life with her must be boring for that poor dog, she thought.

Time to take him into the backyard for a walk. Maybe she should bring his tennis ball and let him chase it a few times. It'd sure make him feel better. Maybe it would even help her shake off the cobwebs of horror, grief and fear that kept brushing her soul and making her want to shiver.

As soon as she picked up the ball, Flash leaped to his feet, wagging his tail like mad. Oh, yeah, he knew what was coming, and the sight of his eagerness made her smile.

"Let's go," she said and headed for the back door. It was nearing midnight, but Flash was good about not barking, so running around for ten minutes or so wouldn't disturb the neighbors.

It was not until she reached the back door and opened it that she realized something had changed tonight. She could not make herself cross the threshold. The night seemed like a huge, solid wall, holding her back.

Panic attack, her mind registered. God, it had been a while. What the hell was going on with her this evening? It was as if whatever progress she had made over time had been stripped from her.

Then Flash, right beside her, growled into the darkness.

Chapter Seven

Cadell heard the call come in when he was halfway home. He turned his vehicle around immediately, lit the roof lights and hit unsafe speeds.

When he pulled up near Dory's house, there were two other cars, lights swirling around the neighborhood. They were collecting a crowd on the surrounding porches. He ignored them, only one thought on his mind.

They let him through and into the house. Dory sat rigidly on her couch, Flash on guard in front of her, holding two city cops and a deputy at bay. No one was going to get near her as far as Flash was concerned.

"Hey, Cadell," said Dan Casey, the deputy. "Ms. Lake said her dog growled at something in the backyard. We didn't find any sign of intrusion."

"Dory. Dory!"

She looked at him, and a shudder ran through her.

"Tell Flash to play. We're here."

She nodded jerkily. "Flash. Play."

At once the dog eased up but remained watchful. Damn, that one had been well trained, Cadell thought. Thoroughly attached to Dory, too.

As Flash relaxed, so did the other officers. They all had a healthy respect for a trained guard dog.

"So what happened?" he asked Dory.

"I don't know. I was taking Flash out back. I figured he needed a walk and a little play. Almost as soon as

I opened the back door, he started growling. I figured I shouldn't ignore him."

"Good decision," Cadell agreed.

"But I didn't mean to cause so much trouble."

"No trouble at all," said one of the city cops, Matt Hamilton. "That's what we're here for. Besides, I agree with Deputy Marcus here. Never ignore your watchdog."

A short while later, the others left, promising to take another turn around the backyard and the alley behind before they left.

Cadell remained. Dory looked at him. "I'm sorry," she said again. "You must have been nearly home."

"Doesn't matter." There was an ancient wood rocker across from the dubious sofa, and he decided to sit in it.

"Would Flash have reacted that way to an animal? Maybe a cat or another dog?"

"He shouldn't, but I could test it for you tomorrow if you want."

She shook her head. "I'm sure you have a life to take care of, and not just me. You've been wonderful, but…"

"But what?" he said. "I don't get to choose how I spend my time? Or are you telling me to get lost, that I'm bothering you?"

She gasped. "I didn't mean that at all."

He smiled. "Good, because I'm going to look around out back myself, then I'm camping here tonight. Got an extra blanket?"

He watched her struggle before she answered, and he guessed she was struggling with herself.

"Kind of an overreaction?" she said finally.

"I don't think so." Unfortunately, he figured he was going to have to tell her about George before long. Problem was, how much did it mean that one convict had dropped off the radar? He was quite sure it happened all the time. The fact that he couldn't get tabs on George's whereabouts didn't mean he was headed this way.

But tonight…tonight he was feeling that a little more honesty was needed from him. She had a right to know what he knew and what he suspected. She'd already set off the red alert when Flash growled, and he was quite sure Flash hadn't growled without a damn good reason.

That was what was getting to him. He looked at Flash, a dog he knew intimately and had been training for a while. The dog's growl wasn't meaningless, and he didn't ever want Dory to think it was, no matter what it signified.

"Lock the front door," he said finally. "I'm going to get my flashlight and look around."

"But the other police already did that."

"I'm sure they did." He pulled up one corner of his mouth in a half smile. "I'm also sure they did a good job. They're all fine officers. This is for me, okay?"

He guessed she got it, because she nodded and locked the front door behind him when he went out to his car. For now he didn't pull it into her driveway, just got his flashlight and other gear.

Because something had disturbed Flash.

FLASH HADN'T BEEN the only one disturbed by something out back. Dory still felt the way the night had seemed like an almost physical wall when she'd tried to walk him. How she froze on the threshold and couldn't move.

She wondered if Flash had been reacting to her and her swift change of mood. Maybe her apprehension had leaped to him. He seemed amazingly sensitive to her moods.

She looked at him now as she sat on the couch waiting, and he wagged his tail lazily, just once. He appeared relaxed.

"Maybe I imagined it," she said to him. "It was the weirdest thing I've ever felt. I wish you could tell me why you growled."

But he couldn't talk to her, although his gaze never wandered from her and his ears were at attention, twitching this way and that as if he were gauging every sound. Probably even sounds she couldn't hear. How could he look so relaxed yet still be so alert?

"You spooked me as much as that crazy feeling," she told him. He didn't seem the least abashed.

She sighed and leaned back on the sofa. Okay, so something had troubled him, too, but it probably wasn't that weird feeling she'd had. Cadell might believe he wouldn't react that way to another dog or a cat, but what about a coyote? They probably came into town sometimes. Or even a rabbit or snake.

As for her, she'd probably smelled something. A faint odor she'd noticed only subconsciously. Something that put her off. A whiff on the breeze. Maybe Flash had smelled the same thing.

Regardless, she was fairly certain that Cadell wasn't going to find anything amiss any more than the earlier cops had. She wondered if she were losing her marbles at last, then realized the dog had backed up her experience.

Okay, she wasn't crazy. So what the hell had happened?

A car pulled into her driveway, and Flash stood. Apparently he didn't need to be told to guard constantly. Except when he was chasing his ball or playing tug with her, he seemed to be on duty all the time. Quietly, but always alert for trouble.

Which, she guessed, was probably why people had taken up with dogs in the first place.

The knock on her front door brought her to her feet. She twitched the curtain back a bit and saw Cadell, so she unlocked the door and opened it.

He stepped inside, his big flashlight still in hand. He just shook his head as he closed the door behind him and locked it.

"Nothing?" she asked.

"Nothing anyone needs to worry about." He looked at Flash. "I'd be happier if I knew what made him growl, though."

She hesitated, fearful of the response she might get. For so long after her parents had been killed, people had regarded her with pity and had openly talked about how she wasn't right and might never be right again.

Even at that age, they were talking about her mind. Her mental state. Unfortunately that had lingered with her as another fear, making her distrust *herself.*

"Let's go get something to drink," she said. "Maybe leftovers if you're hungry. If you plan to spend the night, I may do some talking."

She was surprised to see the warm smile spread over his face. "I'd like to listen."

As simple as that. She just wondered if she'd have the guts to speak.

THANK GOODNESS FOR MICROWAVES, Dory thought as she began reheating the leftovers from the dinner he'd brought. She'd probably have starved without one as often as she forgot to prepare a meal for herself. Sometimes weeks went by while she lived on raw veggies and frozen egg rolls. Some diet. Maybe Betty was right to be concerned about her.

Cadell put the remains of the two salads together on the inside top of a foam container. It could have been embarrassing to expose how little she actually had—a couple of plates, a few mugs, two glasses, cheap flatware—but Cadell didn't seem the least disturbed.

Maybe he'd roughed it when he was younger, she thought. But she had no excuse for this except disinterest. She made enough money, she had plenty socked away…she didn't have to live like someone who was just starting out. But she really didn't care most of the time. She wanted only what she truly needed.

Her extravagance, and it was a big one, was technology. Yes, she needed most of it for work, but not all of it. Some of it was purely for fun, or to satisfy her interest in the technology. Which, she supposed, made her a geek or nerd or whatever the current name was.

They sat at the table, and Dory started out by avoiding the things she'd been thinking about. Her usual style. Even she recognized her misdirection for what it was. Cadell probably did, too. He'd certainly proved to be very savvy so far.

"So how are the ostriches doing?" she asked.

"They're fine. I'm beginning to think they're indestructible."

She glanced up from her plate, forgetting that she was almost afraid to look at him because of the strong response he evoked in her. Longings, feminine longings buried for most of her life, stirred around him with increasing pressure. "Why?"

He shrugged. "Because they're an exotic species I know next to nothing about. Sure, the vet gave me some instructions, but they're even out of the usual for him. It's amazing that my ignorance doesn't seemed to have harmed them any."

"So they're tough."

"Like you."

The words caught her between one breath and the next, and for a few seconds she simply could not inhale. Tough? "I'm not tough," she insisted when she could find her voice. "I'm a wimp. I'm so scared you and Betty decided I needed a guard dog so I could sleep at night. And there's probably no good reason for me to feel this way."

He stabbed his fork into a cherry tomato but didn't say a word. Giving her time to find her own way, pressuring her not at all. His hands looked so powerful, like all the rest of him. She hated to imagine what he must really think of her. He was a kind enough person to try to help her out, but he probably figured her for a nut. And maybe she was.

Taking what was left of her courage in her hands, she blurted, "It wasn't only Flash's growl."

His head snapped up, his dark gaze fixing on her with total attention. "What do you mean?"

"It's crazy."

"Everything about this, all the way back to the murder of your parents, is crazy. I'm not dismissing anything. What happened?"

"Me," she admitted. "I may be the reason Flash growled. I mean…" God, how could she explain this? Words didn't seem to fit it right. "I couldn't make myself go out that door. I was taking Flash out to do his business, maybe run around the backyard a bit, and I froze. It was like…like…" The words at last forced themselves past her resistance, past the tightness in her throat. "Like the night turned solid. Into a wall. I couldn't move."

His gaze narrowed slightly. "Did you hear something? See something?"

"Not that I was aware of. It was just as if this force held me back. Then before I could fight it or push past it, Flash growled. I turned tail and called the police. But maybe he growled because of me. Maybe my crazy fear reached him."

She swallowed hard. There, she'd said it. If he suggested a butterfly net, she wouldn't blame him. She studied her plate, unwilling to read his reaction in his face.

"Has the night scared you before?" he asked calmly.

"Occasionally. Sometimes it seems threatening, but not all the time. Because running out into the night was what saved me back then. It's not like the night itself was ever a source of my terror. At least not enough to worry me or anyone else."

He pushed the salad aside and reached for his drink. "The night frightens lots of people. Understandably. We're vulnerable then. Atavistic response that probably goes back to our cave days, if not earlier. As a species, we're not night dwellers."

"You make it sound so ordinary," she protested. She didn't feel what had happened at the door was ordinary. As a measure of her mental state, it was probably a big red flag.

"I'm just saying that all by itself, fear of the dark is common, and it can become very strong sometimes. We might not even realize what triggers it. But it's not crazy."

"Maybe not," she answered, hearing the flatness of her own voice. She wondered why she was fighting his kindness. Did she *want* someone to tell her she was nuts?

"When you were really little, did you ever wonder if there might be something under your bed?"

She sighed, thinking it wasn't the same thing at all. "Of course."

"I'm pretty sure there was something under *my* bed."

His choice of words startled her. "You still think that?"

He smiled faintly, and she glimpsed it when she darted a quick look his way. "Not anymore. But for a long time, I jumped out of my bed. Far enough away that nothing could grab me. Now, just because there wasn't anything there in the daylight doesn't mean there wasn't in the dark. Reason doesn't work on that one, because we're programmed to have a sensible fear of the night."

"But this was different!" she protested.

"I believe you." He sighed and shook his head. "I guess I'm not being clear. I used to *jump* out of my bed so nothing could grab me. Nothing on earth could have convinced me to put my foot on the floor right beside my bed. It was *real*. What you felt when you tried to go out the back door was real. I don't know what triggered it, but something did, since this isn't common for you. Maybe it's being in a new place. Maybe it's knowing George is out there free now. I can't tell you, but I *believe* you and what you felt."

She swallowed again, then reached for her soda to wet her dry mouth. Her tongue and lips kept sticking. Then she came back to the important question. "Could my fear have made Flash growl?"

"It's possible. Not likely, but possible. Sensing your fear should have put him on high alert, and he should have remained quiet. No, something else bothered him, but it's anyone's guess."

She faced the grim possibility yet again. "So something out there disturbed us both."

"Evidently." He rose and began to gather up the remains of the meal. "Do you want to save any of this?"

It had been pretty well picked over. She shook her head and watched him cross the small kitchen to her wastebasket as he dumped in everything that was left. Then he rinsed their plates and flatware she had brought out for the leftovers, placing them beside the sink.

Drying his hands on the towel she kept hanging from the oven door handle, he leaned back against the small counter. "I'd suggest you move your equipment to my place, but that would only isolate you more if something worries you. I can hardly say you won't be alone there, can I? But I can put my bedroll here and be around when I'm not on duty. There are always the neighbors to help out here."

She knew the offer was meant kindly, but she stiffened anyway. "I've been living on my own since college."

"I'm sure. But George was in prison then. Things have changed a bit. I wish there was some way I could assure you that he's on his way to Brazil or some desert island, but I can't. So you're going to be worrying for a while."

"But it's so *stupid*!" she said vehemently. "*Stupid!* There's no reason for him to look for me. I know that. All these years he never tried to get in touch with me. Not even a letter from prison. Why would that change now? My fears are irrational. Even I know that."

"I don't know about that." He tossed the towel on the counter, then pulled his chair around the table so he could sit closer and take her hand. His grip was gentle, holding hers on his denim-clad thigh. "You saw your brother in the midst of an act so heinous that most people can't even adequately imagine it. You found the monster—it wasn't under your bed, and it wasn't your imagination. Why wouldn't you be frightened of him? You know what he's capable of."

She shook her head a little, although she wasn't disagreeing. His grip felt so reassuring, like a warm, strong lifeline. She'd like to bury herself in that grip.

"Then top it off with finding your whereabouts on your company's website today... That was hardly reassuring."

It was true. Seeing that had not only infuriated her, but it had frightened her. She'd come here to hide from George, not to have him directed practically to her doorstep. "Maybe I should leave. It's probably too easy to find someone around here."

But as soon as the words escaped her, she felt craven. Run? Again? She'd run once, but she still had as many fears, as many nightmares. She couldn't run from herself. She needed to face down the monster that had been pursuing her in her dreams for a quarter century.

Cadell hadn't spoken a word, but she squeezed his hand tightly and hung on. "I'm not running again. It won't do a damn bit of good. I'm carrying my brother around inside me. No escape."

"I don't have any idea how you get that monkey off your back," he said. Gently, he squeezed her hand in return. "But I agree about not running again. And we may be a small town and a sparsely populated county, but people notice strangers. People have noticed your arrival, but it was clear you're a friend of Betty's. He wouldn't have that going for him if he shows up here."

She looked at him, sinking into his dark eyes. They offered something warm and reassuring, welcoming. He made her feel as if he cared about her. Which she guessed he did, since he'd been talking about spreading his bedroll here indefinitely. "If you stay here, won't that cause talk?"

"Nothing that worries me. If it worries you…"

She quickly shook her head. "No. I was actually thinking about you, not myself for a change."

That made his eyes dance a bit. "Just keep your dog in line, lady. I really think he'd have gone for me earlier if you had resisted me holding you in any way."

She blinked, surprised. "But you trained him!"

"Which may be the only reason he didn't spring. He was certainly thinking about it." He nodded toward Flash, who appeared to be snoozing across the kitchen doorway. "He knows he's yours now. Pretty happy about it, too, from what I see."

Then he turned back toward her and astonished her into complete stillness by leaning into her and brushing a kiss on her lips. "More where that came from, if you ever want it," he murmured as he pulled back.

The maelstrom that had been whipping her about was nothing compared to what he unleashed in her with that butterfly touch of his lips. All her life, because she couldn't trust, she'd refused to let anyone get close to her. When an attraction began to grow in her, she had squelched it mercilessly.

"Cadell," she breathed. God, she wanted more, a whole lot more.

He shook his head slowly. "Not now. Not when you've been feeling like a punching bag. Besides, I want you to be sure it's what *you* really want. I don't think you know right now."

She could have felt rejected, but she didn't. Much as she wished it otherwise, he was taking care of her yet again. Remembering what he'd said about his marriage, she guessed he had some trust issues, too. What a pair.

He thought waiting was better. Given her current state of mind, she couldn't disagree. She really did feel all mixed up inside. Strong as her desire for him seemed to be, she couldn't be sure it wasn't just part of the tangled mess she'd become since she'd heard that George was going to be released.

"I'll hold you to that," she said, feeling spunky for

the first time since she'd seen the website and read the riot act to her fellow team members.

He smiled. "I'm counting on it."

SHE DID HAVE an extra pillow and a couple of blankets, and she gave them to Cadell, although she couldn't imagine how he would sleep comfortably even on the rag rug on the living room floor. He seemed dubious about using the couch, and she didn't blame him. Every time she sat on it she was aware of how it creaked.

"You know," she said, "I'm going to stay up and work tonight. You could use my bed."

"Nope. I'll be just fine, and you might actually want to sleep at some point."

She should have been exhausted after the emotional turmoil of this day, but she felt keyed up, almost antsy. Maybe she wasn't really sure the monster hadn't been in her backyard. Although he couldn't possibly have gotten here this soon, could he?

She paused as she started to leave the living room on her way to her office. Cadell was spreading a folded blanket on the floor for his mattress. Dimly aware that despite the food she had just eaten, she was growing light-headed, she ignored that for a moment. More important things concerned her than her routine low blood pressure.

"Cadell?"

"Yeah?"

"How fast could George get here?"

He finished laying out the blanket, then straightened, standing with his hands on his narrow hips. "Depends."

"On what?"

"Well, when a prisoner is released, he's got nothing. And by nothing, I mean *nothing*. They give him a bus ticket to get back to the town where he was arrested. It's nonrefundable. If he has any ID at all, it's his inmate ID. They may give him the address of a halfway house, but basically..." He hesitated. "Unless a prisoner has a friend or family member on the outside, he's going to find life pretty hard for a while. A few bucks in his pocket, maybe a place to lay his head, and no real way to get a job or help. Hell, they can't even get temporary assistance without ID of some kind."

She faced him, leaning against the doorjamb. "That sounds brutal."

"It can be. Those who don't have someone to turn to often wind up sleeping under bridges or at a shelter. If they're lucky, someone will be willing to help them get all the paperwork together to get a new Social Security card, a state ID. Only then can they really start to look for work."

"That sounds like a great recipe for recidivism."

"It is, for long-term inmates. You go in for two years, you might well have access to all that stuff. But after twenty-five...it's hard. Most of them weren't arrested with a Social Security card to begin with. It's gone. Driver's license? It expires, and these days thanks to the new Homeland Security rules, to get it replaced or renewed, you need a birth certificate, proof of residence, Social Security card…you get the idea. It's definitely not easy."

Part of her was seriously disturbed by that news, in a general sense, but when she thought of her brother, she was glad it wouldn't be easy for him to get going. "So it might take George a while before he can even buy another bus ticket?"

"Maybe. Like I said, I don't know his resources. Maybe he made a friend or two on the inside who are willing to help him right now. Or he might find another way to get his hands on money."

From the way he said it, she suspected it wouldn't be legal. And she needed to get to a chair soon. She gripped the doorjamb.

"I'm sorry I can't offer more reassurance," he said after a few beats. "If he's resourceful, he'll manage somehow."

"But there's still no reason he would want to find me."

She saw him hesitate visibly. "Dory?"

"Yeah?"

"Have you considered that half of your inheritance would have been his if he hadn't been convicted?"

"Of course I have," she nearly snapped. "My godparents put it in a trust. They set aside everything but the proceeds of the house, which were used for me to go to college. They told me the rest was my retirement fund, or for help if I ever got disabled. They set me up well for the future, but I can't touch it."

"But does he know that?"

"He should. My godparents told his lawyer when they did it. I think they thought it might protect me from constant pleas for money from him. If he thinks he'll get his hands on a dime, he's in for a shock. Even if I die, he can't have it."

"Maybe he thinks he can make you change that."

And that, she thought, would indeed be enough for him to hunt her down. It was her last cogent thought. Too much, too weary, too light-headed, and the last flare of anger did her in.

WHEN SHE CAME TO, she was lying on her bed, Cadell hovering over her. Flash had jumped up to lie right beside her. Tentatively he licked her cheek.

"Welcome back," Cadell remarked. "Are you eating enough? Should you see a doctor?"

She shook her head a little. "I've always had low blood pressure. Good for my health, but I can pass out easily."

"Well, that was scary," he said frankly. "I almost didn't catch you in time. Pet your damn dog, please. He's worried."

He sounded aggravated, but she didn't feel it was directed at her as much as the whole situation. Cadell struck her as a protector by nature, and right now he must be feeling next to useless.

The inheritance. She'd believed she was protected by the trust, but in an instant she realized that could be a reason for George to want to find her. What if he thought he could make her change it? To demand his share. She rolled over, wrapping her arms around Flash. "Cadell? Is there some way I could just send him money?"

"Yeah, if anyone had any idea where on earth he's gone. And what if it's not enough?"

Her mouth turned even drier and she closed her eyes, holding onto Flash for dear life. She didn't need Cadell to spell it out, but she said it anyway. "He probably thinks he's my legal heir."

"Unless you did something to change that."

"He isn't. The way the trust is set up, he can never have a dime. But what if he doesn't realize that?" Fear seized her then, running across every nerve in her body like a horde of stinging ants. She'd never know why George had killed her parents, but now she knew why he might want to kill her.

The monster was coming for her. There was no longer any doubt in her mind.

ANY HOPE OF sleep had fled. Her blood pressure had returned to normal. Dory tried to push herself into working, but instead she remained on the bed, Flash stapled to her. Across Flash, on the other side of the bed, Cadell had stretched out. Flash kept himself firmly between them, as if he'd made up his mind. Cadell had even had to negotiate permission to lie down.

But now here the three of them were: man, woman and dog, the humans staring at the ceiling, the dog watching everything. His eyes roved restlessly, remaining on duty although there was no need.

Dory rubbed his neck. "Sleep, Flash. No point in you staying up worrying with me."

Not that he seemed to understand. If he did, he didn't care. She sighed, letting the evening sink in the rest of the way. So George *did* have a reason to seek her out. Given what he'd done to their parents, it didn't require much imagination to think what he could do to her if he thought he could get money.

"He used to love me," Dory said quietly, little more than a murmur.

"George?" Cadell asked.

"Yes. He always took such good care of me. Unlike many older brothers, he never treated me like a pest. When he was out for the evening, he'd come back and sneak into my bedroom to leave some little treat on my pillow. Sometimes I'd wake and see him and he'd smile and put his finger over his lips. No noise."

Closing her eyes, she could see that so clearly, and the memory tore at her heart. She'd loved him so much, as much as a seven-year-old could. What had gone wrong?

"Why no noise?" Cadell asked when she didn't speak for a while.

"Our parents were strict. At the time I assumed he didn't want me to get into trouble for making noise when I was supposed to be sleeping. But maybe he was protecting himself, too. I don't know. I wasn't supposed to come downstairs after I was sent to bed. But that night… God, I wish I hadn't broken the rule!"

"Me, too," he said. "I wish you'd never seen that."

She felt the bed move, and the next thing she knew he'd reached across Flash to lay one of his large hands on her upper arm.

"This dog may be good at his job, but right now he's an impediment," Cadell remarked, a tremor of amusement in his voice, surprising her. "So consider this the best hug I can give you."

"He's hugging me, too," she answered, feeling a slight lift to her spirits. A lot of hugs, something she'd been missing in her life since her godparents had died. Almost immediately, her mood sank again.

"Do you really think he'd come after me for the inheritance? Even though his lawyer should have told him it was in trust? That when I die it goes to a charity?" she asked, figuring that, like it or not, she needed to address the possibility directly. Hiding from it wouldn't help anything, and she'd been hiding from a lot for a long time.

"I don't know what he knows," he said honestly. "It's possible he thinks you can change the trust. Or that he'd be the heir anyway. It's mostly still there from what you said."

"Even if I could access the trust I wouldn't. Another way I'm weird, I guess. I didn't want to…"

"Profit from the murder of your parents. I get it."

She sighed. "Like I said, weird. They had insurance policies to make sure their kids were taken care of if anything happened. Would I feel the same if it had been a car accident?"

"I don't know," he answered honestly. "That's a

question for you, but I don't know how you could answer it. That isn't what happened."

She turned onto her side, throwing her arm across the dog, too, and her hand landed on his waist. "Flash sandwich," she remarked. Not that the dog seemed to mind a bit. "You're a cop," she said a little later, her mind flea-hopping around from one item to the next. No rhyme or reason that she could determine yet.

"It's been rumored."

"You know something about people like George."

His answer was clearly cautious. "Something."

"I don't expect you to explain what he did to our parents. I'm just wondering…what did all those years in prison do to him? Could he be worse now? More dangerous?"

"I don't know," he answered frankly. "That long in prison… I can't say. I *do* know that as men get older, they're less likely to commit crimes. Less recidivism among men who are past their midthirties. On the other hand…" He just let it trail there.

"He could have gotten angrier," she said, feeling as if a stone were settling into her heart. "Meaner. It could have made him worse."

He didn't reply.

She spoke again after a minute. "You don't have any idea how much time I've spent trying to figure that night out, to understand what made George do that. It wasn't the George I thought I knew, but I was so little. I knew he was fighting with our parents, but my mother told me once that it was just his age, and he'd grow out of it."

"Often true," he said quietly.

"So what made him so different?" The question seemed to erupt from her very soul. Sitting up slowly, testing whether she'd get light-headed again, she found her feet and headed for her office, Flash right on her heels. Cadell wasn't far behind.

Then she did something she'd never done before: she shared her 3-D rendering of the murder scene that night.

"My God," Cadell whispered.

"This is what I saw. The thing is, once I put all this stuff in, I can turn it around. I can see it from different angles. It doesn't help me to understand anything, but I keep looking for answers. There aren't any. What do I expect? That some ugly demon will suddenly appear in my rendering and I can tell myself that my brother was possessed?"

She closed the image and swiveled the chair to look up at him. "I need to learn to let it go. I thought I had, until word came about George's release. It's like someone opened the floodgates on a dam. It's all coming back as if it were yesterday." She twisted her hands together. "The brother I used to love is gone. I need to face that. I need to face the fact that if he could do that once, he could do it again."

"Dory..."

She shook her head. "My brother is a murderer. I have no reason to think he's not the same person who stabbed our parents. Who cut my mother's throat. And you're right, if he thinks I still have some of that inheritance, he'll want his share. Because if there's one other thing I remember clearly about him, it's how frequently he snuck into Mom's purse or Dad's wallet and took money. Probably for drugs, I don't know. But he was never above stealing. I didn't like to think about it then, and I guess I lost that in the detritus of what came later. He was a thief. Never to be trusted to begin with."

She shook her head as if trying to wake herself up. "I've been trying to connect two pieces of a different puzzle. Trying to fit parts together that never fit to begin with. I don't know why he was often so kind to me when I was little, but that was only a piece of him."

Cadell cleared his throat. "Would you have tattled about his thievery if you hadn't liked him so much?"

She drew a sharp, long breath that seemed to carry ice all the way to her soul. "Maybe. I knew it was wrong."

He didn't say any more, but he didn't need to. Suddenly those pieces snapped into place, and it was painful. Those cherished memories of the before time, as she thought of it, turned black and drifted away like dead leaves.

In an instant it all became painfully clear. She *did* have a reason to be afraid. Her brother was capable of using her and God knew what else if he didn't get what he wanted.

Her breathing broke, and scalding tears filled her

eyes, trickling down her cheeks. "Years ago," she said brokenly, "my therapist tried to tell me that he was a manipulative psychopath. I refused to believe it. I should have. I should have!"

When Cadell's arms closed around her, she grabbed his shirt with her hands and hung on for dear life. Adrift in a sea of ugly discovery, she needed an anchor in the storm.

CADELL HELD DORY for a long time. While he'd been suspicious that she might have valid reasons to be afraid, he hadn't expected anything like this to emerge. For her to suddenly see her childhood in a very different light had to be wrenching in the extreme. He'd heard the love in her voice when she'd spoken of how George had treated her before the murders. That had just blown up in her face.

How much can one woman take? he wondered. He also wondered if she needed a lot more help than he could provide. Maybe he should call Betty in the morning, get Dory to talk to her.

Damn, Dory was isolated. He understood it was by choice. She was a self-proclaimed hermit. But it remained there were times in life when you needed someone else, someone to lean on and talk to. He had buddies he could share almost anything with, but this woman had no one except Betty. Maybe that was enough, but after tonight he wasn't at all sure.

She had warned him she didn't trust, but she had trusted him with an amazing amount of information about herself and her brother. Because he was a cop and might understand?

Being a cop didn't make the horrors understandable. All it did was build necessary walls of self-protection.

But another question seriously troubled him, and when her tears quieted and began to dry, he kept his arms tight around her, as if he expected her to try to escape. Maybe he did. But he had to ask.

"Why'd you make that graphic of the murder scene?"

At once she stiffened against him. As he'd suspected, she pressed a hand against his chest, trying to push him away.

"Do you think I'm sick?" she asked, her voice raw. "Is that what you think?"

"I just want to understand." Not exactly true. He'd heard her say she studied it trying to find some answer, but it was frankly macabre, and he needed to know the reason behind it. It would tell him so much about Dory.

She breathed rapidly but stopped pushing against him. "Why? Because my psychologist taught me to do it."

"What?" He was startled.

"You heard me." Her thickened voice managed to grow angry and a bit sharp. "I couldn't talk, remember? So she had me draw pictures. Any kind of pictures. I drew that night over and over again. It seemed to help. So she encouraged me to keep doing it as long as I felt a need."

"Apparently you're still feeling a need."

He felt her shudder, and her hand, flattened against

his chest from pushing at him, fisted and grabbed his shirt. "It's a different kind of need now. And I don't keep redrawing it. I finished that rendering over five years ago. It's a snapshot of what's stamped in my mind forever. When I was a kid, it was a way to express. You have no idea how many sheets of drawing paper got torn by crayons as I expressed my feelings from anger to terror to sorrow. It was a violent expression for a while."

He rocked a little, wishing she weren't still in her chair. The floor was hard beneath his knees, and this certainly wasn't the world's most comfortable hug. He wasn't ready to let go yet, though. Something was happening tonight. Something inside Dory had opened up. He damn well wasn't going to make any move that might shut her down.

"Police wish they had such good renderings of what a person saw at a crime scene," he remarked after a while.

"It's what I saw. What I *think* I saw." She relaxed a bit against him, tension easing out of her. "Who knows how accurate it is. I don't. Even though I think I couldn't possibly have forgotten or changed a single detail, I probably did. Memory is a funny thing."

"Yeah," he said quietly. Five witnesses could tell five different stories and believe them, even when disputed.

"Anyway," she went on, "until recently I hardly ever looked at it anymore. Then there I was beating my head on the question that didn't have an answer. Looking into my memory for some clue by looking at the image. I don't think I need it anymore."

"Really?" That startled him, and inadvertently he loosened his grip on her. At once she pivoted away from him, facing the computer where just a few minutes ago bloody horror had been displayed. She brought up a list that looked like file names, highlighted a few then hit a key. Another key, confirming the deletion, and they were gone.

"I don't need it anymore," she said quietly. "Problem solved. The psychologist was right. He's a manipulative psychopath. He manipulated me when I was a kid, and given that psychopaths don't outgrow it, he probably hasn't changed for the better. Maybe he got smoother, but nobody could supply him with empathy. It's impossible."

He stood, wincing as his knees shouted at him, then pulled the other, more battered, desk chair over from the corner so he could sit beside her. He didn't know whether all this was a good sign or a bad one for her. Her psychologist had diagnosed George as a psychopath, but had her psychologist ever interviewed George? Was the diagnosis simply based on the things Dory told her? What if it was wrong?

But cautious as he might be about things like that, it remained they couldn't afford to assume George wasn't exactly that: a manipulative psychopath. He'd met plenty of them in the course of his career, people who were simply incapable of any genuine feeling for another human being. Some were good at pretending. Quite a few never got in trouble with the law and were very successful because they were also very smart.

Then there were the others. The stone-cold rip-off artists and killers. Oh, so charming, but dead inside.

She turned her head toward him and said abruptly, "How did you know about my inheritance?"

He stiffened, watching the matchsticks of the bridge of trust they had just started building waver and maybe begin to tumble. "I looked up the murder after I gave you Flash."

"Why didn't you mention it before tonight?"

Yup, he thought, he'd blown it. So he might as well light the final fuse. "I also checked on George's whereabouts. He vanished from the halfway house two nights after he arrived there, and his whereabouts are currently unknown."

"And you didn't think I should know that?"

"Honestly," he said, rising, "I wasn't sure you needed to know. Why add to your fear unless it became necessary?"

"Then what changed your mind? Why should I trust you enough to let you sleep in my house?"

He'd shattered their fragile trust, but he didn't want to add to it by getting into a fight about it. Time to go. "What you told me about him. Good night, Dory. I'll keep watch from my car out front. You know where to find me."

With every step away, he kept hoping to hear her call him back. She didn't.

A PSYCHOPATH. As suspicious as Cadell was of long-distance diagnoses, the more he thought about it, the more he thought that psychologist had been right. As Dory had said, it brought the puzzle pieces together, matching at last.

If George was indeed a psychopath, then trouble was on its way. Standing on her front porch, he considered what he and the rest of law enforcement around here might be able to do. Sure, strangers stuck out. But George might be smart enough to stay in the shadows once he saw how small this place was. Heck, he could probably figure it out by looking up this area online.

Being a psychopath, he had no limits on what he would do. He'd proved that once before. Now, if he felt Dory had taken his inheritance, he'd do anything necessary to get it back. Coming out of prison with nothing might have exacerbated an old resentment, a feeling he'd been robbed. While Dory wasn't responsible for that, she still held his entitlement. What if he believed her death would leave it all to him, trust or no trust?

If they were lucky, he'd call and demand his share. But Cadell's neck itched with a certainty that he wouldn't do that. Whatever he'd been denied by his parents that had brought him to the point of a vicious murder, he had showed his stripes. If murder was the easy way, he'd take it.

Wishing vainly that he could locate George was a waste of time. The guy had finished his sentence. Nobody now had a reason to keep tabs on him, so unless he crossed paths with law enforcement because of a misdeed, he might never pop up on the radar again.

Damn it! What the hell had he been thinking? Sure, he wanted Dory to feel safe. She desperately needed it, and that's why he'd given her Flash. The woman had been terrified, and while at the time he'd thought she'd never really need Flash, the dog would be a comforting presence and protector to have around.

Now here he was standing in the ruins of a budding relationship with a woman who'd quite frankly told him she couldn't trust and preferred to be a hermit.

Well, he'd pushed himself into her life, and now it was time to back out. Let her be. She had Flash to look out for her.

Forgetting Dory for the moment, he sat on the top step, wished he hadn't quit smoking ten years ago, and thought about everything he knew.

The image on her computer was stamped into his brain now, like a piece of evidence, and he wasn't particularly concerned about whether her memory had been faulty. It still told him things.

So, George had been stealing from their parents and subtly manipulating Dory to keep her quiet about it. He might have taken more than money out of a purse or wallet, leading to the fights Dory had mentioned. Creating tension.

But that scene in the kitchen, the wounds Cadell had read about…that was no impulsive murder. The heat-of-passion argument had been enough to prevent a life sentence, but Cadell was no longer buying it.

Rising, he climbed the step and rapped on Dory's door. "Dory, it's me." Then he opened the door and stepped in.

Flash came charging at him.

Chapter Eight

"Flash, no," Dory snapped just before the dog reached Cadell. She hadn't put him on guard, but she honestly wasn't sure if he was attacking or greeting. "Stay."

Flash immediately halted, and only then did she note that his tail was wagging happily. Then she looked at Cadell, part of her still burning angrily and part of her honestly glad to see him.

She was annoyed that he hadn't told her he knew something about George that she didn't, but on the other hand...well, Cadell was obviously protective.

"I thought you'd gone," she said.

"I didn't get all the way off your porch. The cop kicked in. Is there any chance you can recover that image of the murder? Because I'd like to look at it."

She hesitated. She'd had the sense that he'd been horrified that she'd drawn such an image in so much detail. "What changed?"

"Like I said, the cop kicked in. Some things struck me, so I'd really like to study it."

She nodded slowly. "I can recover it." She paused, then asked, "Want a soda?"

"Any chance of coffee?"

The faintest of smiles lightened her face. "Of course. Just let me start the recovery and then I'll make it."

WHEN SHE REACHED the kitchen, she had to grip the edge of the counter and lean on it. Her knees felt weak, and she was shaking from head to toe. Had it mattered so much to her that he'd walked out? That he'd come back? Hadn't she been mad at him?

But all of that had vanished in the contradictory realization that he hadn't left. Now he wanted to see her rendering of the murder scene. Maybe she'd been wrong in thinking that she had repelled him with it.

Drawing several deep breaths, telling herself she was overreacting, whether to Cadell's return or the idea that there was a good reason for George to seek her out, she didn't know. Too much. She'd lived with too much for a long time.

The coffee didn't take long. She seemed to remember that he took it black, so she carried a mug to him. She didn't want any herself. She was already wound up and simply relieved to have stopped shaking.

The picture once again filled the screen, every detail clear.

"You can turn it?" he asked, then thanked her for the coffee.

"Yeah, but you have to understand I couldn't see it from any other direction, so you get the reverse of what you see here, plus the other side of the kitchen as I recall it."

"Every little bit helps. Can I rotate it myself?"

"Not easily." She pulled a chair over, and he scooted to one side while she called up a menu. She highlighted a box from the graphics software. "The problem with this is you're not really moving the picture, you're moving cameras around it. It can get awkward."

He nodded and picked up the mug, drinking, his gaze intent on the screen. "Turn it ninety degrees, if you can."

Well, that was easy enough. She hated this view, though, looking straight at her brother as he stood over their parents. It didn't look like him, of course. He was a morph, but she knew exactly who it was—an unrealistic face didn't change that.

He spoke. "The kitchen behind him. That's what you remember should have been there?"

"Yes."

"Okay, give me another ninety in the same direction."

She did. There was the dining table, the doorway, the little girl standing at the foot of the stairs. Her brother partially blocked the view, though.

"Do you have a drawing of the kitchen without him in it?"

"Of course. That's where I had to start."

"Can I see it?"

At least the shakes were gone, she thought as she reached for the mouse and switched to another image. The kitchen. Empty. The way it should have been that night at that hour.

"A back door," he muttered. "A knife block all the way over there, with the table in between."

"In between what?" she asked. Her heart was accelerating as she wondered if he'd seen something there that she hadn't.

He rubbed his chin and leaned back in the chair. It

creaked, but he said nothing as he continued to stare. Finally he stabbed his finger at the screen, pointing out the knife block. "All the knives are there."

"Well, of course," she said. "Until he used one."

"I want you to look at this whole picture, Dory. The whole thing. For now just use your imagination to put the figures in it."

"Okay." That wasn't hard to do, considering that she'd looked at it until she hardly needed it anymore.

Her parents lying on the floor between the table and a wall of dish cabinets. George standing over them.

"The police report said he killed them with a ten-inch chef's knife," he said.

"Yes," she whispered, then opened her eyes in spite of his instructions.

"From that butcher's block."

"Yes."

He swiveled, and suddenly she was fixed by his gaze. "This was premeditated."

IT HAD TURNED into a night of shocking revelations. She didn't even want to know how he'd reached that conclusion, not at first. Giving up all thought of sleep and peace, she headed for the kitchen and got herself a cup of coffee. Cadell wasn't far behind, refreshing his own mug.

"I'm sorry, Dory. But the more we know about him…"

"I get it," she interrupted, not caring if she was rude. "I get it."

Oh, yeah, she got it. He was saying that her brother hadn't been overcome by a blind rage, driven to an act he might never otherwise have committed. He was saying George had intended to kill them. That he'd planned it. Who knew how long he might have been planning it? Subtly bribing her and making her love him, then reinforcing their parents' dictum that she mustn't come downstairs after she was sent to bed.

Considering how many rules he'd broken, it was weird that he hadn't wanted her to break any.

"God," she whispered.

"Maybe you should sit down. I don't want you to faint again."

"I don't know if I can, and anyway I think my blood pressure is through the roof right now. Cadell, how can you be sure?"

He nudged her over to the table until she was sitting. "If you can stand to, think about that kitchen. How likely is it that he could have taken both your parents by surprise if he'd gone to get a knife? He'd have had to round the table, go to the knife block and come back around that table… Don't you think at least one of them would have run at that point? Getting the knife was a deadly threat, not some innocent act like getting a glass. The fact that they're lying beside one another… He was already armed. He took them utterly by surprise, and he knew exactly how he was going to do it."

Somehow she had moved past feeling shocked. In place of all her fears was the feeling that she was receiving repeated blows yet again, anger surging in her.

Fury at George. Fury at what he had done and the scars and terrors he had left her with.

She closed her eyes, clenched her fists and wished he was there to scream at, to pound, to tell him once and for all that he'd killed part of her, too.

But George didn't care. He'd never cared. *Manipulative psychopath.* The brother who'd been so sweet to her had merely been using her. Then a strange calm came over her, leaving her feeling as if she were standing outside herself, observing from miles away.

"I have my answers now," she whispered.

"So it seems." He was quiet a moment, then said, "I guess I should leave. I've given you enough shocks and bad news for one night. You're going to hate the very sight of me."

Her eyes snapped open. Her voice emerged tonelessly. "I'm going to have nightmares if I sleep. I'm going to wake up screaming."

He stood there, his face creased with concern, his hands opening and closing as if he didn't know what to do. "Do you do that often?"

"A lot since I heard about George's release. I can feel it coming, almost like I'm already half-asleep. He's going to stalk my dreams."

"God," he muttered.

She looked down as she felt something on her thigh. Flash. He'd rested his head on her, his eyes peering up at her.

"Cadell?"

"Yeah?"

"I can't stand to be alone in the dark when I wake up screaming."

He shifted, then slid into the chair he'd pulled closer earlier. "I'll stay. I told you I'd stay tonight. I just figured after what's happened, you might want me gone. Being the bearer of bad news and all."

Still feeling oddly detached, she lifted her gaze and studied his face. "You didn't tell me anything new. Not really. Well, I *did* get angry when I found out you hadn't told me those things. Then you left."

"Not exactly," he admitted. "Didn't make it three steps. But I reckoned you felt betrayed, and for someone who says she can't trust… I figured all the bridges between us had been burned."

She shook her head slowly. "For a minute or two… Well, I'm glad you came back. And I'm glad to know for sure now about George. No questions left. You answered them. All the time I stared at my representation of that awful scene, I felt like there was an answer there somewhere. You found it."

"I'm sure that's thrilling you," he said tautly. "Good old Cadell, bringer of more bad news. I'm a great one for making people feel worse."

Her head jerked up at that. A sliver of feeling pierced the cold detachment that had overtaken her. "Brenda?"

"What?"

"Did your ex make you feel that way?"

She watched him consider it for a few minutes. "Yeah, in part. But being a cop brings a lot of that on, too. How many times have I had good news to deliver? Not many."

"I never thought about that," she confessed. "Never thought about what it could do to you and other police officers. My memory of the police is all warm and good. They took such good care of me back then. All of them. I've never forgotten it."

"I'm glad you feel that way."

Impulsively, surprising herself, she reached out for his hand and wrapped hers around it. "You're a good man. I keep thinking about how awful all this has been for me, but tonight can't have been fun for you, either. I'm surprised you came back after the way I reacted earlier."

He shrugged slightly. "Like I said, the cop kicked in. You told me you'd been looking for answers in that graphic, and while I was out on the porch doing a decent job of beating myself up for sacrificing your trust, I thought about what you'd said about seeking answers in that picture. You have an artist's eye, but I have a set of cop's eyes, and a thought occurred to me. I'm sorry it was so bad."

"The whole thing was bad." Some of her detachment was easing, and she wished she could hang on to it. She doubted she was ready to start feeling anything yet. Unfortunately, she knew she would. She always did. That night had been haunting her for over a quarter century. If she could have become ice, she certainly would have done it by now.

"Look," he said after a moment, "you really need some sleep. For that matter, so do I. It's awfully late."

So much had happened since he'd arrived with dinner that time had flown. Looking at the clock, she started. "Wow. Don't you have to work in the morning?"

"I'm off tomorrow. Maybe, if you can find time, you and Flash could come out and check on the ostriches with me. I'm certainly going to need a shower and a change."

The smallest of smiles cracked her frozen face. "Sure. Why haven't you named them?"

"The birds? Because I don't want to get attached. I'm trying to get rid of their ornery butts, remember?"

He turned his hand over and tugged her gently. "Bed. Flash will keep me in line. If you have a bad dream, I'll be right there."

At last, she nodded and felt the tension that had been building for hours let go. She wouldn't be alone. And while she was sure Flash would protect her, he wasn't the same as having someone right there she could talk to. During the time with Betty, she had learned how much that could mean. Since moving into this house, she had realized how much she missed having someone there.

Then his words struck her. "Why should Flash have to keep you in line?"

He just laughed. She felt a few more cracks in the ice that was encasing her, because she understood that laugh.

For the first time in a long time, she hugged something special close to her heart.

GEORGE CUSSED HIMSELF for a fool. He'd gotten all the money he needed off that woman, and she hadn't slowed him down much. It was everything else that was slowing him down.

Things had changed since he'd gone to prison. He'd been shocked to discover that he couldn't even buy a bus ticket without ID. The last thing he wanted was a record of where he'd been. The bus company might have accepted his prison ID—they had when the prison sent him home—but even if they would, he didn't want anyone to be able to trace his movements. Not with what he had in mind.

Of course, that gave him an idea. Walking boldly into the bus station, he asked for a ticket to Miami, and while the clerk hesitated a moment when seeing his prison ID, she didn't hesitate long. He walked out with a ticket to Miami, a false trail already started.

Now he just had to figure out how to get to that place in Wyoming. Once again, he walked to a different town. The outdoors still felt too big to him. He wondered if he'd get past that. Anyway, he felt better when surrounded by houses and trees. They cut the sight lines to something more reasonable. But from what he knew of Wyoming, he was going to have to get used to wide-open spaces quickly.

The next town had a small library, but that didn't mean they were without computers or the internet. He made his way to one of them without having to show a card or other ID and set to work. If they didn't want people to walk in and just use the machines, if they hassled him...well, they had books, and he was pretty sure they didn't have a problem with people browsing the books.

But no one harassed him the least little bit, and he began to do his research on Conard County.

An hour later he was wondering what had drawn Dory to a place like that. It was the ends of the earth. Hardly any people, nothing to do, really. The main town, Conrad City, was a cow town, if that. The plus was that she'd stick out and be easy to find. The minus was that so would he.

Leaning back as far as the chair would let him, keeping his hand on the mouse, he tabbed between pages. One gave him the stats about the place. Another gave him a reasonable map, although he was sure plenty of minor roads probably didn't show up. The third gave him photos. Beautiful mountains, a worn-out town and plenty of wide-open spaces.

He had no way to know if Dory had moved there on her own or if some guy had drawn her there. Her personal life was a closed book to him. Crap, she didn't even have a social media account under any possible name he could cobble together for her.

It hadn't always been like that. That was how he'd learned she'd become a graphic artist and worked for some company. Then everything had shut down ten years ago. As if she'd gone underground and wanted to stay there.

It didn't make any sense. What was she afraid of? He'd still been in prison, and anyway, he'd given her absolutely no reason to fear him.

If only she hadn't come downstairs that night. She'd loved him back then. He'd made sure of it. Made sure that she worshipped him more than their parents, that she was his ally and kept his secrets. Then she'd broken the rule and come downstairs.

Even so, she had no reason to fear *him*. No reason to think that her loving brother would come after her with murder in his heart. He'd *always* been good to her.

It did seem suspicious that her location had changed on the company's website right around the time he was released. But it had changed back. What if it was just a mistake? Because why the hell would she go so far out of the way?

"Sir?"

George looked up. A middle-aged woman smiled at him. "I'm sorry, but you've been using that computer for over an hour, and we have other people waiting."

He smiled, calling on every bit of charm and sexiness he owned. No point in making himself memorable. "I'm sorry. Let me just shut down my search."

"Oh, take a few more minutes," she said, smiling in answer. Her cheeks even flushed a little. "I'll explain you're almost done."

As she walked away, he wondered if he should chat her up a bit, maybe spend the night with her. Then his memory flashed the image of the wedding ring she wore.

Nope. He'd have to find a different flophouse.

He closed out his search, erased the search history and rose, heading for the door. He gave the librarian another smile before he stepped out into the sunny morning. The library was on a wide boulevard, and for a moment he froze, overwhelmed by the space. Then he gathered himself and began to stroll down the sidewalk, glancing in shop windows, a handsome man just past forty. He liked seeing his reflection.

All the while his mind kept ticking things over. The change of address, changed back. Too coincidental. Why the middle of nowhere? Because she was afraid, after all?

When he'd seen her standing in the kitchen, he'd tried to reassure her, telling her he'd gotten rid of the bad man. Had she believed him? She should have, but a lot of years had passed, and he'd spent them in prison. Maybe she believed his conviction more than she had believed him. Certainly something in her had snapped. He'd never forget the way she ran from him and stood in the street screaming her fool head off. The sound had frozen him, had thrown all his plans into a mixer, and in the end he hadn't had the time he had planned on to clean himself up, get rid of the weapon and lay a false trail.

If she'd just stayed in bed… She'd never told their parents that he was stealing from them, even though she'd seen it. In the end she'd never told anyone anything about that night, as far as he could tell. Hell, she'd stopped talking entirely. His lawyer had been good about keeping him informed. The freaking lawyer thought he was worried about his sister. Idiot.

He'd kept tabs through that guy, loosely, of course. The years she spent with her godparents, a couple he'd never cared for. The trip to college when briefly he'd been able to follow her on social media. But then, for no apparent reason, she'd dropped out. Gone. Canceled her accounts.

He still wondered what the hell had brought that on. Maybe someone had been bothering her. Anyway, she'd apparently never picked it up again. She was almost as far off the radar as he was.

The idea made George smile. Maybe he could just make her disappear. Who'd be worried about it? Her coworkers? If she had friends, he hadn't been able to find out. Not even that damn lawyer could tell him, and finally the guy had gotten impatient, reminding George that he was not on retainer and while he'd been doing favors out of kindness all these years, he was through.

Bastard. George sometimes thought he'd take care of that lawyer once he'd settled matters with Dory.

With a start, he understood he'd reached the end of town. He hesitated only a minute before deciding to just keep going, heading west. He'd been warned that hitchhiking was illegal, but that didn't mean someone wouldn't pick him up. He looked innocuous enough, clean, not too big, carrying a backpack over his shoulder. No one would guess that a slender guy like him could be trouble.

Which was just how he wanted it. He'd used his exercise periods to stay lean. Fit, but lean. Bulking up like so many of the guys did only made a man look like potential trouble. George didn't want to frighten anyone.

For now the only weapons he needed were his good looks, his smile and his tongue.

EVEN THOUGH IT was late, the morning sunlight almost hurt Dory's eyes as she opened them. She needed to get some curtains in here.

Then she realized she was alone. At once she turned over and saw that both Flash and Cadell were absent. Reaching out, she touched the covers and felt warmth. They hadn't been gone long. Then she heard sounds from the backyard and saw that Cadell was running Flash through his paces.

She sat up and stretched until joints popped. No nightmares. None. Not even a hint. She'd just had the best sleep she'd had in weeks, maybe a month.

Feeling better than she had in quite a while, she slipped out of bed and headed for a shower that would make her feel even better.

When she emerged freshly dressed in a light T-shirt and jeans with a towel around her blond hair, she stepped outside to watch Cadell and Flash. They'd passed the work stage and were now at the play stage.

She smiled as she watched the dog jump for joy each time Cadell threw the ball. To be so happy…

Before her thoughts could take a downward spiral, Cadell called Flash to heel and came toward her. "You slept well?"

"Like a rock. It was amazing. That hasn't happened in a while."

"Good news, then. When you're ready, we'll go out to my place. I *do* have something there besides two ostriches and a dog kennel."

Her smile started to widen, then hitched. "Who's taking care of the dogs?"

"They are," he said simply. "I never know when I might have to be away for an extended period, so I have a very modern kennel. It feeds and waters them."

"And the ostriches?"

He laughed. "I hope they got all the insects out of the corral."

His cheer was contagious, and she liked it. Before long they were heading out to his ranch with Flash in the cage in back. He seemed excited, as if he knew he was going to visit his dog friends.

Dory wondered what was happening inside her. After last night's shocks, shouldn't she be more upset? Instead she felt as if she had been freed in some way. Maybe Cadell had given her some of the answers she'd been looking for. Maybe now she felt she knew what she was facing, rather than wondering.

But she was sick of her own fears this morning, and she shoved them aside. George's release didn't mean she couldn't still have an enjoyable day. In fact, now that she thought about it, she was appalled at how much power she'd given her brother over her. She'd allowed him to haunt her for years. Allowed him to terrorize her sleep and dreams. He didn't deserve that right.

Lifting her head, she looked to her left and drank in the mountains. At midday they looked a little hazy, the greens very dark except for lighter patches here and there. She wondered if she was looking at different trees or if that was the dappling of sunlight.

"Cadell?"

"Yeah?"

"After your divorce...did you find it hard to trust?"

He snorted. "Oh, yeah. I got distrustful of women, and I got distrustful of myself."

"Why yourself?"

"Because before that I thought was a fairly decent judge of character. Afterward, not so much. Which was probably a good thing for a cop."

She turned a little in her seat so she could look at the side of his face. "How so?"

He paused as he steered them into his rutted driveway. The truck began to jolt. "Because it's not possible to really judge a book by its cover. In my line of work, making that mistake can be deadly. I guess I figured out that before you can trust someone, you need to get to know them. You need to see them in stressful situations, not just dates where everything is fine. If I ever marry again, I'll want to know how a woman reacts when the toilet overflows."

The quiver began deep inside Dory, and seconds later emerged as the heartiest belly laugh she'd had in ages. "The toilet?" she gasped finally, wiping an errant tear from laughing so hard.

"Well, it could be something else," he allowed. "But I think you get my drift."

She did indeed, but it was still funny, and she couldn't stop grinning. She imagined him with a clipboard ticking off boxes as a harried woman worked on a toilet.

"Are you keeping a checklist?" she asked.

"Not consciously. But that's the best way I can explain it. People change under stress. I kind of think it's important to know how they change. Every life has problems that have to be dealt with. I'd prefer someone who can deal."

Which ruled her out, Dory thought, wondering why it should matter. He'd seen her under stress, and she didn't think she was getting any gold stars from him. Afraid of nightmares, of being alone? Afraid of her brother? Turning herself into a hermit because she trusted no one easily? How was that truly coping with anything? She was a mass of defense mechanisms.

She sighed, imagining him filling out his checklist when it came to her, or worse, writing "Failed" across the sheet.

Oh, well. She might not pass his tests, but that didn't mean she couldn't enjoy the day. Even if George were somewhere close, he'd never find her out here.

Chapter Nine

Cadell had left the ostriches in the corral, which was also electrically fenced. They'd done a good job of scratching up the place looking for food. Leaving Dory to get out of his vehicle in her own time, he headed for the pen. The two birds came running.

"Yeah, you guys know who feeds you," he said. Before he let them in, though, he had to dump feed in their trough. No way was he going to let them get close. He'd learned his lesson.

He opened the gate into the pen and stepped back as the two birds entered. He didn't know if he wanted to confine them again just yet, so he left the gate open.

Dory had joined him, Flash at her side. "Man," she said. "They moved fast!"

"They didn't even get up to full speed. Quite amazing birds...at a distance."

He was pleased when she laughed again. He'd gotten the feeling just before they finished the drive that something had darkened her mood. Well, not really darkened. Not that bad. Just a kind of sadness, he guessed.

Which under the circumstances needed no explanation. He was pretty impressed with how well she'd handled last night's revelations, especially the one about the murder being premeditated. She probably had been fighting that thought for years, unwilling to believe that her beloved brother was capable of it. Much easier to believe he'd lost his temper in a big way than to imagine him plotting the entire thing.

He led her along the fence. "See the wire fencing inside the wooden corral? Courtesy of my father and the ostriches."

"What was your dad like?"

"An honest, decent, hardworking, churchgoing man. Respected by his neighbors. A good example for any kid."

She looked toward him. "Why'd you leave?"

"Youthful wanderlust, I guess." He sighed and shook his head a little. "I didn't think I was cut out to be a rancher. It about wore my dad to a nub. Same thing every day and worries that never quit." He shook his head a bit, leaned his arms on the fence and lifted one booted foot to the lower railing.

"It's hard to remember what I was thinking back then," he said. "I'm sure it made perfect sense to me. I tried staying for a couple of years, but my dad didn't stop me when I took off. He was already winding down the operation here. Cattle are expensive to raise, and he wasn't getting enough when he sold them. I sometimes wonder if he didn't think I'd be better off doing something else."

"Maybe he did," she said quietly. The breeze was blowing, tossing her hair, caressing her skin gently. A beautiful day. "Then you come home to the ostriches."

He laughed easily. "Yup. And don't think I don't wonder if he planned that. He knew me well. I wouldn't leave animals uncared for, and he probably knew just how much difficulty I'd have getting rid of this pair. What a way to get me back to my roots, but he sometimes had a strange sense of humor."

"They're quite a joke," she remarked, watching the two strange-looking birds eat ravenously. "I know they're birds, but…"

"Too big," he agreed. "Dinosaurs."

"I've heard people can ride them."

He laughed again. "No, thanks."

He studied her for a few minutes before turning his attention back to the mountains that loomed over one side of his ranch. She seemed tentative. After starting the day in a mood so good it surprised him, she had retreated a little.

"I wish I could have met your father," she said.

"Why?" It occurred to him that she'd never really had a chance to know her own father or mother. After all, a child of that age would have only a few memories and very little knowledge about the adults in her life.

"Because the person you are tells me something about him." She astonished him with a small smile. "I'm sure he was every bit as good a man as you said."

Quite a compliment coming from a woman who'd frankly told him she didn't trust easily. Although saying something like that was hardly a matter of trust.

A bark from the kennel area drew his attention.

"Flash!" Dory said and then laughed. "He must be feeling forgotten. He wants to play with his buddies."

"Let's go let them out, then." He paused only to lock the ostriches in their pen.

The summer-baked ground was hard beneath their feet, the remaining grasses dry and crackly. Out back where the kennels resided, however, the ground softened and greened because of how often he had to spray down the concrete. Each kennel opened onto a small, individual outdoor space so the dogs didn't start feeling too cooped up, but right now they were all at the front, watching Flash, who was prancing right up the middle of the dog run.

"I could almost swear he's taunting them," Cadell remarked.

"That dog is capable of more expressions and feelings than I would have believed," she answered. "You have a lot more cages than dogs. How come?"

"It varies, actually. I don't just train police dogs. I work with service dogs and even family pets. But mainly my job is being the lead K-9 officer and trainer. Anyway, every now and then I might have eight or ten dogs here."

"That'd keep you busy."

"It sure does. Some training is far more intensive and time-consuming that other types." He walked down the row, opening the kennels and letting the dogs free. At once they entered a joyous chase all over the unfenced acreage, to the ramshackle barn and back. Their joy was infectious, and both Cadell and Dory smiled as they watched.

"So," he said, risking it, "who took care of you afterward?"

He watched her suck her lip between her teeth, and

he regretted spoiling the mood. Still, he needed to know her better. Wanted to know her better. He had not the least doubt there was more to this woman than the graphics designer and the frightened little girl.

"My godparents," she said after a moment. "They'd been good friends of my parents for a long time, and I knew them somewhat. Better than foster care, I imagine."

"The only judge is you. Did you feel loved?"

"They tried. I can't have been easy. Like I said, I didn't talk for over a year. They took me to therapists and doctors. But even when I started speaking again... well, I told you I don't trust people. All the way back then, I lost my trust. It had to be hard on them. They gave me so much, and when I look back I realize I gave them very little in return."

"I doubt they were doing it for what they could get out of it, Dory. I'm sure it was more about what they could do for you. Anyway, Betty became your friend. How did that happen?"

Dory's face lightened. Relief flooded him. He hadn't ruined today for her. Enough that he'd ruined last night.

"She was my English teacher my sophomore year of high school. How well do you know Betty?"

"In passing. We're not tight, but we talk from time to time. Why?"

"I just wondered if you had any idea of how persistent she can be."

At that he laughed. "I've heard about it."

Dory's smile grew. "She was persistent with me.

I don't know why, but for some reason she wouldn't let go. She kept working on me, talking to me in odd moments. Finally she started inviting me and my godparents to have dinner at her house, and then they reciprocated and... Well, she never gave up on me. Even after I went to college, she'd drive over on a Saturday and take me out to lunch. Like water dripping on stone, I guess." She gave a little laugh, and her gaze met his. "I don't know when or how it happened, but she became my friend. My only friend. After my godparents died, Betty was the only person I had left."

He nodded. He was beginning to get a real clue about how truly alone this woman was. "What happened to them? Your godparents?"

"A tornado," she said simply, then directed her attention back to the mountains.

God, he thought. She'd been through a hell of a lot. The murder of her parents, the betrayal by her brother, then the loss of her godparents in an extreme act of nature? Without giving it a thought, he stretched out an arm, wrapped it around her shoulders and drew her to his side.

He wanted to find a way to express how bad he felt for her, but he suspected she wouldn't want that. She had made peace with most of her life, as far as he could tell. With everything except her brother. Anyway, sympathy didn't make up for the losses. So he offered what comfort he could with his touch.

After a couple of minutes, she surprised him by turning toward him and resting her cheek on his chest.

"I'm such a mess," she said. "I don't know why anyone puts up with me."

"I don't think you're a mess."

She shifted a little against him. "How can you say that? I told you I can't trust. I'm afraid so much of the time…"

"I don't blame you for either. What your brother did would make it hard for anyone to trust again. As for being afraid… Well, he's a coldhearted murderer, isn't he? I wouldn't want to run into him any more than you do."

A thin laugh escaped her. "No machismo?"

"I'm not going to promise you something I have no right to promise," he said firmly. "I'm here for you, but that doesn't mean I can guarantee anything about your brother or your safety. All I can promise is that I'll do my damnedest."

Slowly her arms wrapped around his waist. He had to close his eyes against the sudden surge of passion. It had been simmering since he'd met her, and he'd been dumping cold water on it because that was probably the last thing she needed or wanted. Some problems were too big to be answered with a roll in the hay.

"Thank you," she said. "Thank you."

"For what?" He couldn't imagine.

"For being honest with me. Last night you told me things you knew I didn't want to hear, and now today you're not making wild promises. Not that I'd believe them."

The dogs were beginning to tire from their romp

but weren't quite ready to quit yet. He stood there with one of the most beautiful women he'd ever met and wondered if he were capable of letting his own guard down enough. She freely said she found it hard to trust. Well, he did, too.

They made quite a pair. A hopeless one.

THE SURPRISE HE had promised her came in the form of Betty. She arrived midafternoon while Cadell was still checking the dogs for ticks.

"I need some help," she announced.

"Betty!" A smile bubbled up in Dory. "What's wrong?"

"Nothing. I just have a car full of food this young man asked me to buy, and I'm danged if I'm going to carry it all myself."

"One more dog," said Cadell, looking up. "What did you do? Shop for an army?"

Betty put a hand on her hip. "Clearly you don't shop for groceries here often. Shopping for two or three is impossible. So I hope you have some freezer space."

Dory felt a spark of curiosity. "Why is it hard to shop for small numbers?"

"Because an awful lot of people hereabouts have large families or shop for a couple of weeks at a time so they don't have to drive into town."

"Then what do you do?"

Betty's eyes twinkled. "I flirt with the butcher. He'll give me a single steak or chicken breast when that's all I want. However, he wasn't there today, so I had to get what's available. We could feed six or eight easily."

"I've got the freezer space," was all that Cadell said.

For a second, Dory had feared one of them would suggest inviting others over. She knew Betty wanted her to meet people, but not right now. Please, not right now. She was still feeling too stirred up.

"I'll help you," she said, ready to follow Betty to her car. She could at least do that much.

"I'll be along in just a minute," Cadell said. "Just go ahead and put everything on the table. You know your way, Betty, right?"

"That house isn't so big I could get lost," Betty answered drily. "Yes, I've been here before, that time you had that barbecue." She eyed Dory. "The man is popular. I think a couple of hundred people showed up for that one. He had to send runners to the store for more burgers."

Cadell's laugh followed them. "It was the free barbecue," he called.

"More like the ostriches," Betty commented as she led the way around to the trunk. "They're the talk of the whole damn county."

"I've been missing you," Dory said truthfully as she helped Betty pulled the reusable bags from the trunk.

"You'd miss me a whole lot less if you weren't always working," Betty retorted. "Those times I dropped in, I felt like I was interrupting."

"You probably were, but that doesn't mean I minded."

Betty laughed. "I'll keep that in mind." They

climbed the front steps together. The house had a wide porch, and the front door was unlocked. "How are you and that dog making out?"

"I love him," Dory said simply. "I hardly have to tell him what to do. He seems to know."

"Cadell's a great dog trainer, from all I've heard." Betty turned left into the kitchen. She'd been right: the house wasn't big enough to get lost in. They put the bags on the kitchen table—much bigger and sturdier than Dory's—and began unpacking.

"You sure went to town," Dory remarked as she began to stack items. "You could feed an army!"

"Hardly," Betty said. "But I figured you could take some of this home with you. What have you got in your refrigerator? Soda. In your cupboard? Popcorn. Really, Dory."

"Hey, it's not as bad as all that."

"Right," Betty drawled.

Cadell joined them and separated out the three steaks, the potato salad and the bag of frozen broccoli. "For our meal?" he asked.

"Yeah," said Betty. "Then I'm thinking Dory can take home most of the rest. I just don't want it to spoil in the meantime. Have you seen her refrigerator?"

Cadell grinned at her. "An awful lot of raw vegetables. And soda pop."

"Ha."

Dory smiled. "What is this, a conspiracy to feed me?"

"Somebody has to. You'd forget to go to sleep if you could."

Being here with the two of them made Dory feel even better than she had upon awakening that morning. The not knowing must have been making her feel worse than knowing. Cadell had certainly answered one of her most pressing questions about the murder, and that was a relief, too. The whole thing had been so horrific. Facing her brother's capacity for such acts removed all the doubt that had plagued her over the years.

He'd never loved her. He'd used her. And he'd use her again if he could. Strange as it seemed, that made her feel stronger. Made her feel that she could face the moment when he came for her. If he came for her.

Or maybe it had simply taken love out of the equation, relieving her of the torment of wanting to understand because she still remembered loving George. Her unwillingness to face what he really was in the hope that he wasn't that bad. Yet terrified of him at the same time.

A royal emotional mess, she thought as she helped make dinner. Clarity, after all that, was welcome.

Not that it killed her fears. She suspected they'd always be there if George was on the loose. But at least she didn't have to feel guilty and confused because he'd loved her as a child. He'd never loved her at all.

AFTER A DELICIOUS DINNER, they settled on the front porch with cups of coffee to enjoy the late-afternoon breeze.

"So," Betty asked after a while, "any news on George?"

"Not exactly," Cadell answered when Dory remained silent. He looked at her, not Betty, as he spoke, hoping he wouldn't see shadows chasing across her face again. So far her face remained untroubled. "He went to a halfway house in his hometown, then vanished from it after only two days. There's been no trace of him since. I'm keeping my ears and eyes on it, though."

"Good," said Betty. "Although if that man has a lick of sense, he'll stay far away from her."

Dory turned her head. "Why do you say that?"

"Because you're the one person he can reasonably be expected to contact. Does he think no one would be watching out for you?"

Betty had a point, Cadell thought, but she was reckoning without knowledge of the inheritance. George had been willing to steal to get what he wanted, to lie to keep it secret. And to kill when something went wrong. Right now he was out there with nothing. Why would he pass up a chance to go for all that money if he thought there was any way to get it? Cadell seriously doubted he would just show up and ask for it. After all, Dory knew who had murdered their parents. Why would she turn all that money over to him?

If he'd been keeping tabs on Dory, he probably knew she hadn't married and didn't have children. But even if he hadn't, he wasn't above taking out her whole family to get what he wanted. Of that Cadell had not the least doubt. He'd seen it in that graphic Dory had made. Clear as crystal.

Dory spoke, surprising him. "Cadell says the murder was premeditated."

Betty drew a shocked breath. "How can he know that?"

"Because I made a three-dimensional graphic of the kitchen and murder scene."

"Oh, my God," Betty breathed. "Why? Didn't it just make everything worse?"

"No. I was using it to try to understand. My therapist taught me to draw things I couldn't cope with. It just continued. So I had this graphic."

"Amazing," Cadell intervened smoothly. "She wanted her answers, and it was right there in her drawing or whatever it's called. Clear as day if you knew what to look for. The man's a psychopath, Betty. And yes, as a cop, I would call the murder impossible unless it was premeditated."

Betty leaned over and seized Dory's hand. "How are you coping with this? Are you okay?"

"I'm fine, actually. Knowing is better than not knowing. Especially now that I don't have to wonder any longer if George loved me. He never did. He used me. I can't tell you why, but that makes this easier somehow."

"But you're still afraid?"

"Of course." Dory regarded her from eyes that suddenly looked hollow. "At least there's nothing left to muddy the waters if he shows up, but I think I'll be living with fear for a long, long time."

Cadell ached for the woman. He hadn't thought her

good mood could survive the day, not as last night's blows began to sink in. But he *did* understand what she meant about it being easier knowing George had plotted the murder and had used her. It gave her permission to throw out her last lingering hopes about her brother. It gave her permission to hate him if she needed to.

It gave her permission to do whatever was necessary to protect herself.

He stared out over the rolling plain, the dry summer grasses, the tumbleweed caught on his neighbor's fence, feeling the weight of the mountains behind almost like a physical force. An energy. If they had lived and breathed, he wouldn't have been surprised.

Part of him hoped George Lake would show up here. Part of him wanted to wring the man's neck for all the suffering he had caused Dory.

Another, more sensible part of him hoped George was next seen somewhere in South America.

He didn't feel a lot of hope.

A little while later, Betty stood up. "I've got to get home. Dory, do you want to come with me?"

"I'll take her," Cadell said. "Her dog is here, too."

"Well, don't forget the food. I mean it, girl, you need to eat better. You're too thin already."

Dory gave a little laugh. "That's a matter of opinion."

Betty simply shook her head. "I don't know how anyone can stay that thin sitting at a desk all day and evening. Which means you're not eating enough. I'll say no more…until next time. So it's okay if I drop in?"

"Absolutely."

A short while later, Cadell watched the dust cloud rise behind Betty's small sport utility vehicle. It sat high enough to get over the rough roads around here but was just big enough to carry her, one passenger and her groceries. Putting Flash in there would have been ridiculous. A seventy-five-pound dog wasn't exactly small.

"It'll start getting dark soon," Cadell remarked.

"The mountains really suck the light out of the afternoon."

"I kinda like it. Anyway, let me know when you want to head home. You seemed to enjoy the day."

"I did." She gave him the full force of her lovely smile. "I really did. I didn't expect to, but…well, it was a relief. I suppose it won't last long."

"You never know. You could move your stuff out here if you think you'd feel more comfortable. The thing that bothers me, though, is that you'd be really isolated out here when I'm at work. In town, you can always get help."

All of a sudden, maybe because of the words *in town*, she slammed back to the little girl standing in the street screaming. She'd gotten plenty of help. Out here, no one would hear her scream.

"Thanks, but I'll stay where I am. Generous offer, though."

"Not entirely without ulterior motive," he admitted.

Startled, her eyes widened and she uttered a totally uncharacteristic "Huh?"

He chuckled quietly. "You know I'm attracted to you. Admit it. I've even let you know. From the first moment I saw you, I thought you were the most beautiful woman I'd ever seen."

He could see her cheeks redden. "Don't exaggerate."

"I'm not. It's my personal opinion. You're absolutely beautiful. But it's more than that. The better I get to know you, the more I want you."

He paused, watching a rapid play of emotions run across her face, too quickly to read.

"Anyway," he said, rising. "I don't want to scare you more. Let's pack up the groceries and the dog and get you home. You can decide if you want me around tonight."

"I'd like you to stay with me," she said.

Well, his heart leaped a little at that. *Down, boy,* he said to himself, as if he were one of his dogs. "Okay. Let me pack what I need for tomorrow, check the dogs one last time and then we'll load up."

DORY WONDERED WHY she'd asked him to stay. Flash was a great protector, but for some reason she felt safer with Cadell around. Crazy, since the last people in her life to make her feel at all safe had been her godparents, and it had taken them years.

Cadell brought out his uniform in plastic from a dry cleaner, neatly pressed on a hanger. His gun belt and all those accoutrements went in the back end with what looked like a whole bunch of other law enforcement stuff.

She peered in. "I never saw what was in a policeman's trunk before." About the only thing she recognized was the body armor.

"Not nearly as much as I used to cart in Seattle. There's actually room for the groceries."

He brought Dasher as well as Flash, probably because he needed his dog for work the next day. He'd also brought a sleeping bag.

She couldn't have begun to say why that made her feel cheated. She wanted no involvements, she didn't trust anyone except Betty and she was just beginning to trust Cadell.

No, it was best this way. Having him there would make her feel safer. Any more than that was a risk she didn't yet dare take.

Even if she felt the constant irritant of desire when he was around.

OVER THE NEXT DAYS, Dory and Cadell settled into a routine of sorts. She began working a little less during the daylight hours, instead driving herself out to spend time with him at his ranch as he trained dogs and tended the ostriches.

She thought he'd die of laughter when she told him she'd named the birds Itsy and Bitsy. Well, she was smiling more, too.

Except when she looked out over the wide-open spaces. Deep in her bones, she felt George was coming, that her fear was no figment of her imagination.

Not since Cadell had mentioned her inheritance. People had killed for a lot less money.

A nugget of real anger had begun to burn in her, however. That man had destroyed her childhood, had blighted her life, and now he wanted to steal more. She was sure of it. If he'd cared about her at all, he'd have left instead of killing their parents. He wouldn't have taken them from her.

Ergo, he didn't care. Not at all. It was all about George.

The anger felt empowering, reducing her fear bit by bit. She knew the terror would return; it always had. But for now anger was a great reprieve. When she was out at the ranch with Cadell, she channeled that energy into working with the dogs, helping where she could. Daily she grew increasingly impressed with how much labor and patience went into training the dogs. Cadell wouldn't settle for half measures. These dogs would be walking with someone carrying a badge, and no one could afford the least miscalculation or misbehavior.

Most of the dogs were simply eager to please and did what was required of them. They were happy knowing their good behavior would be rewarded by playtime.

But one, a week later, failed the course.

"It's killing me," he told her as they watched a Malinois dash around the backyard. "He's going to have to go."

"Why? Are you going to put him down?" A new kind of horror filled her. She had grown attached to all these dogs.

"Of course I'm not going to put him down." He spoke almost sharply, then softened his tone. "No, nothing like that. But I can't curb his energy sufficiently. He's stubborn, and while all the things I teach these dogs should be fun for them, he keeps rewriting the rules. I'll wind him down a bit, and then he'll be suitable for a pet."

Considering she had been consistently amazed by how hard these dogs tried to please, she was surprised that any of them would fail the course. But when she thought about it, it made sense. One of the other things she'd learned from working beside Cadell was that the dogs had their own quite distinct personalities.

Cadell touched her arm, and a ribbon of pleasure ran through her. "It's okay, Dory. Not every dog is cut out for police work. Or rescue work. Just like some aren't cut out to be service dogs."

That sparked interest in her. "Do you teach service dogs, too?"

"Sometimes. That's a really special skill, though, so I don't do it often."

"I don't get it."

"It's simple. Service dogs need a lot of in-depth special training, and they have to be individually trained to serve a particular kind of companion. It's better to have someone familiar with all that do the job. But service dogs are expensive. Not everybody can afford one, and not everyone can be supplied by a charity. So occasionally, I do it. It's a hell of a lot bigger job than what I usually do. In many cases it's a matter of teaching dogs to do things they don't normally do. Whereas a police or rescue dog…the talent is pretty much innate for that kind of work. It's mostly a matter of directing it."

She laughed then. "And making sure they listen."

He winked and looked back at the corral. The dog was still running around, chasing and tossing the tennis ball for his own amusement. Itsy and Bitsy watched from their pen, their huge dark eyes intent.

"Now watch," Cadell said. "This is part of the problem." He whistled and called the dog's name. The animal looked at him, then went back to the tennis ball. "See? Two months and I still can't get him to come reliably. He'll make a couple of kids happy, but I can't send him out with an officer. *Most of the time* just won't work for them."

Later he persuaded her to stop at the diner for supper, although she wasn't entirely comfortable with being out in public. Dang, she thought, this man was pulling her out of her comfortable hidey-hole whether she wanted it or not.

But she felt safe going with Cadell, which worried her. Was she turning him into another bubble around herself, a safe place that held everything else at bay?

Troubled, she hardly said anything throughout the meal. She put down a hamburger and fries and didn't taste a thing.

She was a psychological mess. Nothing had ever completely sorted her out, but so far she'd managed not to hurt anyone else with it.

After dinner, he insisted on paying the bill, then surprised her again. "Let's go over to the sheriff's office."

She balked on the sidewalk. "Why?"

"You don't think I'm the only one trying to track down your brother, do you? I've asked for some help. I don't know about you, but I'd feel a whole lot better if we could pinpoint his location. Come on, nobody bites, and everyone would like to be sure you're safe."

Her temper flared. "Who gave you the right to discuss me with anyone?"

He put his hands on his hips, tilted his head and simply looked at her. God, he looked good in that blue shirt, jeans snug on his narrow hips, a cowboy hat shadowing his head. So good. Why the hell was she trying to start a fight?

But she hadn't given him permission to make her problems public, and it troubled her that other people knew. Even police officers.

"If you want me to apologize for protecting you," he said, "then I will. But I won't mean it, and you'll know it. So what's the point, Dory?"

"It's having so many people know about me! I don't like it."

"They're cops," he said, an edge of frustration creeping into his voice. "They know how to keep things secret. Not a one of them is going to gossip about you or your brother. Not here, not ever. Unlike the rest of this town, they know how to zip their lips about matters like this."

She couldn't speak, the turmoil inside her was so

great. She felt as if she'd been left exposed in plain sight, tied out like a goat.

"Dory, you can't face this alone. You don't need to."

She'd had enough. She never should have come to this benighted town. Letting Betty talk her into coming here had been a huge mistake. Painful layers had been stripped from her once again. Her privacy. Her small sense of security. Even her coworkers had helped expose her.

George. She should have just hit the road and kept moving on a regular basis. The idea that she could now ever stay in one place seemed like insanity.

Without a word, she opened the back door of Cadell's truck and took Flash out. He'd been sitting in there in a wire cage with the windows open. Now, glad to be free, he jumped down eagerly.

"Flash, heel." She grabbed his leash and hooked it to his collar, then started walking home.

Alone.

Because alone was the safest way to be. The only way to survive.

Chapter Ten

"Damn it," Cadell said under his breath. Had he really done something wrong by trying to trace her brother? Evidently she thought so. But it was the kind of thing he'd have done for anyone as a cop, and usually people were grateful for the interest and possible help.

She was one confusing woman. Life had seriously wounded her, and he wasn't sure that she was able to be truly rational when it came to George. Well, of course she wasn't. None of this was about reason. It was about gut feelings. He ought to know that.

After a moment's debate, he hopped into his vehicle and drove the half block to the sheriff's offices on the corner. A parking space awaited him, and he slid into it a little too fast. Then he walked into the station, where he was greeted by the dispatcher, a new hire who'd started only the month before over the old dispatcher's objections. He gathered that Velma, who'd been with the department longer than anyone could remember, felt she was the only one who knew how to do the job properly, which had caused a parade of new hires to quit over the years. Duty officers had often had to fill in the excess hours. Harriet, the new woman, was at least adequate, although Cadell was already wondering how long she'd last with Velma constant carping at her.

"Gage?" he asked.

"In his office," Harriet answered. "Getting ready to leave."

Gage had an open-door policy, so Cadell didn't hesitate to walk himself back and knock. Gage looked up from the papers he was straightening, his burn-scarred face offering a crooked smile. "Hey. What's going on?"

"Apart from me stepping knee-deep into a pile of manure, nothing. I've got one less dog I'm going to train—wrong temperament. I'll have a couple more sometime next week."

Gage pointed to the chair. "And?"

"The manure, you mean?"

"Obviously."

Cadell didn't want to sit. "Dory Lake is furious with me for bringing you in on her problem, and she's walking home alone with her dog, Flash."

"The one you trained?"

"Yes."

Gage nodded. "Then she should be safe enough." But that didn't keep him from reaching for a radio. Five minutes later he had both deputies and city police officers advised to keep an unobtrusive eye on Dory Lake as she walked home. "Make sure she doesn't know."

The tension inside Cadell eased.

After a moment, Gage spoke. "She doesn't have any reason to trust us, you know. I read her case. Sure, cops took care of her after she ran out of that abattoir that had been her home, but I gather she hasn't trusted much since."

"No," Cadell admitted. "I may have blown it entirely, but I'll head over there in a little while and try to mend the fences."

Gage rocked back in his chair. "That's up to you."

"Meaning?"

"Exactly what I said. If you want to mend fences, mend them. I tried to call earlier, but you didn't answer. It seems her brother bought a bus ticket to Miami. Last week."

"So he's headed the other way."

"Uh, not yet. He never used the ticket."

Cadell closed his eyes. "Hell."

"Misdirection? Maybe. I've asked my counterpart in Florida to keep an eye out for him, but if he never went there…"

"I get it." Cadell stood up. "Thanks, Gage."

"You might not want to wait," Gage said as Cadell was walking out. "Don't give her time to raise the drawbridge over the moat."

Cadell paused and looked back. "You're troubled, too?"

"Let's just say from what I read, I wouldn't put anything past George Lake. Not even murdering his sister. She may have every reason to be terrified."

DORY DIDN'T WANT to answer the knock at her door. She'd been vaguely aware that there seemed to be more than the usual number of police cars on the streets, and one corner of her mind wondered what was coming down.

But Flash's tail told her who was at the door. At the moment she wouldn't have opened it for anyone without knowing who was there. She needed to get a peephole installed, she thought vaguely, but right now there was no threat outside, simply Cadell.

She wasn't sure she wanted to see him ever again. She felt exposed, like a raw nerve ending, and it was his fault. Her past haunted her, not only within her own mind and heart, but everywhere else, it seemed. She'd had to tell her coworkers about her brother, which she'd never wanted to do, and now Cadell had broadcast it. So what if only other officers knew about it? She couldn't manage to hide from it, no matter what she did.

Flash danced a little from side to side, impatient. The slightest begging whimper escaped him. Damn it.

She opened the door at last. Flash did a little happy dance, then immediately sat, realizing he was in danger of breaking his rules. Not that Dory cared. She hadn't put him on duty yet.

Cadell looked somber, standing there with his hands at his sides. "May I come in?"

She wanted to slam the door in his face but caught herself in time. Just because the rest of the world was going insane around her didn't mean she had to, as well. Anyway, she was already crazy enough.

"Sure." She stepped back, letting him pass. Flash wiggled a bit in his seated position, hoping for a pat. He got one from Cadell as she closed the door.

She led the way to the shoddy living room and let him have the couch. She had her doubts about the wooden rocking chair holding him for long. It barely held her.

"I ran into your neighbor out front. Marissa Tremaine. Have you met her?"

What did this have to do with anything? "Not yet." And with the urge to pack up and move on growing stronger in her, she doubted she was going to meet anyone.

"Her first husband was killed overseas a few years ago. She lives in that big house across the street with her new husband and child. It's nice to see her happy again."

Point? She wondered where he was going with all of this. So what if that woman was happy again? Happiness had eluded Dory most of her life. Oh, here and there she'd run into it, but it didn't last long. Somehow it felt disrespectful. All the therapy hadn't changed that, either.

"Look," he said, "I'm sorry I upset you, but I'm not sorry that I spoke to the sheriff about this. All he can access is public records."

Her lips tightened a bit, but she nodded. Public records? Anyone could get those if they looked.

"Anyway, it turned out to be useful. He found that your brother purchased a bus ticket last week from Saint Louis to Miami."

Tension hissed out of her like the leaking of a balloon. "He's headed away."

"We don't know that. The ticket hasn't been used."

That was all it took. Tension once again gripped her, winding around her every nerve ending. "Damn it," she muttered. "Damn him." She looked at Cadell. "He's not stupid."

"Nobody's counting on him being stupid. The sheriff has someone in Miami keeping an eye out for him, but if he uses the bus ticket, we should hear quickly."

"But he could give the ticket to anyone!"

"These days you can't travel by bus without ID. I doubt his prison ID would pass muster for anyone else unless he can find a near-identical twin. Regardless, he found the money to buy the ticket. I'm wondering what else he's been up to."

"Stealing," she snapped. "What he used to do all the time. I'm surprised he's not leaving a string of police reports in his wake. Oh, wait...he's probably being careful not to be noticed. So we really don't know anything."

"I'm afraid not."

But she saw that he didn't really believe this was nothing. No. She closed her eyes. "He tried to lay a false trail. He's coming here."

Cadell didn't immediately answer her. When he did, it was clear he was choosing his words carefully. "We can't know that based on just one thing."

Her eyes snapped open. "Tell me you don't really believe that."

His frown deepened, and he rose from the couch, pacing the small room, seeming to nearly fill it with his presence. She easily imagined that everywhere he went he made rooms feel small. "We can't know that," he repeated. "But it's suspicious enough to put me on alert. I'm sure the sheriff feels the same."

"Well, thank you for that."

He stopped and stared directly at her. "Meaning?"

She'd been extremely sarcastic, and she really hadn't meant to be. Or maybe she had. "Sometimes I feel as if people just dismiss me as crazy. I've felt that way for years. Well, I am a little crazy, I suppose. Untrusting, afraid of shadows…even when George was in prison, I didn't feel entirely safe. It just wasn't something I could explain. I guess I don't need to explain it anymore."

"Of course not. Anyway, I don't think you're crazy. What happened to you as a child was bound to have a long-term impact. I'd be amazed if it hadn't. *Then* there'd be something wrong with you."

Unexpected gratitude filled her, washing away the last of her irritation with him. "I'm sorry," she said finally.

"For what?"

"For getting so mad at you. You were right, you were only trying to protect me. I'm not used to that."

He shook his head a little. "I should have asked you first. I was high-handed, and I know it."

"The cop?" she said, allowing a little amusement to slip into her dark internal places.

He smiled faintly. "The cop," he agreed. "I have this thing about taking charge."

She rose from the rocker. There was little room to put between them, and other feelings began to niggle at her. Among them an overpowering desire for him, to put aside everything for just one night. She'd given in to that urge only a couple of times in her life and had learned how rarely it turned out well. But Cadell…since the beginning something about him had been calling to her on multiple levels. She wanted his friendship, though, and after what he'd said about his marriage, she doubted he'd be interested in anything more. Even though he'd mentioned it…

Her thoughts stuttered between one breath and the next. He'd told her he wanted her. What kind of delusion was she feeding herself now?

"I need a drink," she said and marched to the kitchen for a bottle of soda.

"I could do with something strong," he remarked, following her.

"I don't have anything. I don't like liquor."

"I meant coffee," he retorted. "I'm not much of a drinker myself. I've seen too many problems arise from alcohol. So call me an occasional one-beer man."

She screwed up her face. "No beer for me. I don't like the taste."

"Tsk," he said, but she could tell he was teasing. Someone teasing her was a relatively rare experience. Probably her own fault. After all, she was far from the easiest person to get along with. So many hot buttons, who would dare?

She started the coffee and got herself a cola. She was oranged out for the day. Settling in at the table, with Flash beside her, she sipped from the bottle and thought about her reactions that day. One minute she was enjoying Cadell's company, enjoying the dogs and—dare she admit it—amused by the ostriches, Itsy and Bitsy. Then she'd gone off like a rocket because he'd asked his colleagues to keep an eye out for developments with George.

"Why do you put up with me?" she asked bluntly. "I'm a pain."

"True." He leaned back against the corner while the coffeemaker hissed and streamed black brew. The corners of his eyes, however, were crinkled. "You don't come close to Itsy and Bitsy, however."

"What have those ostriches ever done to you?" Once again, amusement was trying to creep in. She decided to let it.

"They ate two of my favorite hats. Felt. Leather hat bands. Stretched just right to fit my head perfectly. I'm ashamed to admit that not until after they grabbed the second one did I realize it was going to be a continuing problem. I thought about getting a football helmet."

At that she cracked a helpless laugh. "Why did they want the hats?"

"Ask them." He shrugged. "Didn't take them long to shred them, though. The goats aren't nearly so bad."

She straightened. "You have *goats*?"

"Sorta, but not exactly. I pasture them farther from the house for one of my neighbors. I don't need them arguing with the birds or the dogs."

"But the dogs could hurt them, too."

He shook his head. "One of the ways I finish up training is by taking the dogs out to the goat pasture.

A new distraction. If they can follow orders despite the goats, they pass."

She shook head, feeling a smile tickle the edges of her lips. "I thought you weren't ranching."

"I'm not. I've got two birds and I provide grazing for a neighbor's goats. That's not ranching. Ask anyone." The coffee had finished brewing and he snagged a cup from the cupboard to pour himself some. Then, at last, he gave her room to breathe again by coming to the table and sitting.

"The goats amuse me," he said. "Last spring I headed out there with one of my dogs. There were lots of little kids gamboling about, but one of those damn adult goats had jumped up on the roof of the hay shed. I still can't figure out how he got up there. I wonder if he was sick of all those noisy, excited kids. Or maybe he thought he was on guard duty. Anyway, I called my neighbor, asked what he wanted me to do about it."

"And?" She was loving this.

"He said, 'Damn goat got up there, he can get hisself down.' Which he did by the next day."

This was a whole part of the world she'd never been exposed to before, and it delighted her. Most of her life she'd lived in suburban or urban areas, and the last decade or so she'd pretty much become a troglodyte. Her graphics work endlessly fascinated her. It always offered a fresh challenge, and the amount of detail required kept her fully engaged.

But goats and ostriches? Her exposure had been one

trip to a local zoo when she was ten, and she didn't remember any ostriches.

For the very first time, she considered the possibility of remaining here, once her problems with George were behind her. There seemed to be a whole wealth of new experiences awaiting her, something she hadn't thought about in a long time, if ever.

"You know," she said slowly, wondering how she had come to trust him this much, "I've let George deprive me of too much. Even when he was in prison, he controlled my choices in a lot of ways. Made me avoid other people. Made me distrustful." She paused then hit on the underlying truth. "It's time I realized that he hasn't been the one depriving me. I've made all the choices since he went to prison. He's no Svengali, controlling me at a distance."

She sighed and stared down at the table, at the familiar bottle of cola, and took a hard look at herself. "Plenty of people go through terrible things that leave deep and abiding scars. That doesn't mean they quit. I've quit, Cadell."

The chair creaked as he leaned forward and stretched out a hand, palm up. Uncertainly, she placed her hand in his. "You haven't given up," he said.

"What do you call it when I want to be a hermit? Betty's the only person I've let get close to me in my entire life."

"Including your godparents?"

"Including them. God, they gave me so much, and I gave almost nothing back, and now it's too late. There were people in college who tried to be my friends, but I always pushed them back until they quit trying. I've made myself a nice, safe little world, but it's far from complete."

A few beats passed before he responded. "What made you think of that?"

"Goats. Ostriches. Dogs." She shook her head and lifted her gaze to his. "It just struck me—I'm missing so many things by living in my little cave. It's not that I don't enjoy what I'm doing, because actually I do. But there's so much more out there. Maybe I ought to make a little time for it."

"You've been coming out to the ranch and working with me and the dogs," he reminded her.

"It's true. But that's a baby step. Maybe I should meet my neighbors. Talk to that Marissa you mentioned earlier. Meet other people."

"I'm not opposed to that, but I'd suggest you take it slowly."

"But why?"

"You don't want to overload yourself. You're not used to a big social life, are you?"

"I'm used to words on a screen," she admitted. "But maybe that's not enough anymore." Then she sighed. "Anyway, George."

"George?"

"All these ideas about changing my life would be easier to implement if I didn't have him hanging out there like an albatross around my neck." The part of her that had been trying to expand pinched a little.

She felt it happen. "He's coming, Cadell. I think we both know that."

He didn't disagree.

"So all plans are on hold for now," she said. "I've got to deal with him somehow. If he just wants money, he can have it. If he wants me dead…well, I don't think I'm going to let that happen. So I'm going to stop hassling you about everything you do to try to help. I'm just sorry I'm taking over your life."

His hand tightened around hers. "You're not taking over anything. I'm exactly where I want to be."

She half smiled without humor. "Cop?"

"Cop," he answered. "But only partly. I also happen to like you. And yeah, you can be difficult, but who can't? I'm the take-charge guy who'll probably annoy you again. But unless you want to throw me out, this is where I'm staying."

A warm rush of gratitude filled her. "You're a nice guy, you know."

"Don't feed my ego." Then he grew serious. "I mean it, Dory. I'm here because I want to be. And I *do* like you, thorns and all."

"Why is that the sweetest thing anyone's ever said to me?"

"I can't imagine. But it's not sweet, it's just true." He paused. "I'm not one to shine people on. Never have been. If I have a problem with you, you'll know it. And if I say I like you, I mean it."

"Thank you." But even as the warmth continued to remain with her, her mind insisted on jumping around, which wasn't a usual state for her. She could summon a laser-like focus for hours when she needed it, and had long ago learned a reasonable control of her thoughts. That was what cognitive therapy was all about. Which was not to say she never slipped, and the news of George's release had caused a big-time slip. She'd come running to the first offer of a haven like a scared mouse.

But now she was glad she had, because she would have missed a lot if she hadn't.

"You're never going to believe this," she remarked, "but I like Itsy and Bitsy."

He didn't seem disturbed by her change of subject away from him liking her—a pregnant statement, full of possibilities she wasn't ready to consider. Possibilities she somehow knew she was going to hug to herself, because she liked him, too.

"I don't *dislike* them," he answered. "We have a mutually irritable relationship."

"Well, I'm not saying I want to pet either of them." She summoned a smile. "What happened to your mother? You never mentioned her."

"Where did that come from?" But he didn't wait for an answer. "She died shortly after I was born. Some kind of infection."

"I'm really sorry."

He shook his head a little. "I never knew her, never knew what it was like to have a mother. Sometimes I wished I was like other kids, but mostly I just accepted it. My father took good care of me. He worked me hard on the ranch. But he still made space for me to have a social life when I was in high school. I guess I never thought about the work he must have been doing when I wasn't there."

"But he didn't have a problem with you becoming a policeman?"

"If he did, he never let on. I may have mentioned it already, but by then he was winding the ranch down. Swore the land had more value than the livestock."

"Did it?"

"I lease a lot of it, so yeah, I guess. But then I look at those dang ostriches and wonder if they weren't a plot on his part to keep me rooted here. He was a great believer in roots. So am I, I guess. No regrets at all about coming back here."

"Roots." She spoke the word, feeling around it in her mind. "I'm not sure I really had any. Even when I was with my godparents. Uncle Bill, as I called him, was always being transferred. Sometimes we went with him if it was going to be a long stay, and sometimes Auntie Jane and I remained where we were. They did more of that when I was in high school. I guess they thought that was important."

"Wasn't it?"

She shrugged. "I don't know. Like I said, I don't make friends. Well, except for Betty. I met her in the high school in Saint Louis."

"Well, I'm your friend now, so live with it."

He was teasing her again, and she liked it. There was something so normal about it, a normalcy she'd avoided for years. Now that she was trying it on, a piece at a time, she was discovering that it was good.

She was acutely aware that these feelings were just a house of cards that would tumble the instant George arrived, but she couldn't give up these moments.

"He stole too much from me," she announced. Then, with a boldness she exhibited in her work, she rose and came to his side. "You busy tonight, Deputy?"

He looked up at her, his eyes narrowing. "I was planning on being here."

"That's not what I meant." Then she opened the dam she'd built to avoid thinking about what she truly wanted and let the needs pour through her for the first time. She was done holding them at bay. Good experience or bad experience, she didn't care. She was damn well going to have the experience.

"Come to bed with me," she murmured. "Now."

Chapter Eleven

Cadell froze, conflicting emotions welling up in him. He wanted this woman, no secret there, but he was also afraid of hurting her in some way. He wasn't even sure why she was asking so boldly. Every time he'd thought he glimpsed heat in her gaze, she'd concealed it quickly. Even so, just a short time ago she'd been furious with him, and now this? What had brought it on?

Rising, he slipped his arms around her waist and felt a tremor pass through her. There was only one way to know. "Why?"

She closed her eyes and shook her head a little but didn't draw away. "Is this the time for analysis?"

"I'm not asking for analysis. I want a reason. I'd like to know that you don't want to use me to make you forget. I need to be more than that."

"Nothing can make me forget," she whispered. "But I've missed a whole hell of a lot because of that. I want you. I've wanted you for a while, but I kept coming up with reasons to tell myself no. I tried to bury it." Her blue eyes opened and met his straightly. "I can't bury it, Cadell."

He supposed that was honest enough. And from the tightness of her whispered words, he sensed this honesty wasn't easy for her. Why should it be? People talked easily about a lot of things, but sex seemed to be different. He'd also gathered that it was never easy for her to admit her own desires and needs, whatever they were.

Living in a cave hadn't helped her to blossom in many ways. She was a flower in desperate need of some sunshine.

He leaned closer and brushed his lips against hers. "You should know I want you, too. I've mentioned it more than once. But it has to be good, Dory. Are you sure this is the right time for you?"

"There'll never be a right time if I think about it too much. Cadell..."

These could be the tenderest moments between two human beings or they could become an ugly mistake. He wanted her more than he could say, but he needed to protect her, too.

So do that and quit being a jerk. See where it leads. Satisfy her in every way.

And to hell with his qualms. If regret were coming, it was going to have to wait a few hours.

He kissed her again, pushing his tongue a little past her lips until it met the gate of her teeth. Another shiver passed through her, then she let her head fall back and her mouth open. She hadn't changed her mind.

For right now, that was all he needed.

Flash stood up as Cadell swept Dory up into his arms. "Darlin', could you tell your watchdog to stay?"

Dory quickly clasped her arms around Cadell's neck and spoke thickly. "Flash, stay. Guard."

"You could sound like you mean it," Cadell remarked as he easily carried Dory the short distance to her bedroom.

"He better not get in the way," Dory mumbled. "You'd think he'd understand he doesn't need to guard against you."

"He does." He'd made sure of that over the past week. He just hadn't wanted the dog in here, where he might misinterpret something as play to join.

He set Dory down slowly, sliding her along the entire length of his body. She inhaled sharply as she felt him hard against her. No secret about his desire anymore. The pressure even through his jeans made him want to groan. He reminded himself to take his time, to make sure she could savor every sensation. Then thought started to slip from his grasp as she reached down and touched him through the denim.

"Mmm," she murmured.

He had this thing in his head, where he undressed a woman, then himself. Where it had come from, he had no idea, but it now completely vanished. She reached for the snaps on the front of his shirt and ripped them open ruthlessly. Then her soft, small hands began to explore his chest, sending shafts of pleasure through him with each stroke, each caress, even each pause as she learned his contours.

When she brushed over his small nipples, he was unable to repress a shudder.

"You, too?" she murmured. Before he could respond in any way, she'd leaned forward and taken him into her mouth, licking and sucking until the drumbeat in his head grew deafening.

Not only was this woman an angel, she was also a witch. A very talented witch with her tongue. Then she gave him a gentle nip, and he jerked.

He looked down at her, and there was no mistaking that pleased, sleepy smile. "Happy with yourself, huh?" he asked, his voice low. He was now sure he wasn't dealing with a totally inexperienced woman, which removed his last inhibition.

Oh, this was going to be good.

Reaching out, he grabbed the bottom of her T-shirt and pulled it over her head. Amazement grabbed him as he discovered a lacy bra, not at all what he would have expected. Delightfully, it pushed up the globes of her breasts invitingly.

Bending his head, he kissed the top of each breast, then ran his tongue lightly over her skin. A soft moan escaped her. Then, with a twist of his hand, he found the back clasp and released it.

At once the bra gave up its control, but before he could slide it away, Dory did so. She stood before him in the dim light from the hallway, making no attempt to conceal herself from his gaze. Instead she took his hands and pressed them to her breasts, then leaned in again to suck on his small nipples.

As he massaged her breasts, trying to judge her response by her soft moans, he felt her hands reach for the snap on his jeans. So that was how it was going to be?

Thrilled, he reached for her jeans, too. With almost surprising speed, underwear and denim fell to the floor.

Now the damn shoes. He pushed her down so that she sat on the edge of the bed, then squatted to remove her tennis shoes, her socks and the last of her jeans.

A giggle escaped her, surprising him.

"What?" he asked, looking up before attending to his own problem.

"Is there any graceful way to do this?" she asked.

"Yeah. Robes. Negligees. Nudity." But a smile creased his face as he sat beside her on the bed and fought his way out of his work boots and all the rest. He even remembered to grab a condom and roll it on. "Kind of a punctuation mark."

But then she stole his breath by reaching out to close her hand around his erection. "Dory..." Her name escaped him on a choked breath.

"You're a beautiful hunk," she murmured, her own breath beginning to come rapidly. "Can we..."

"Anything," he promised, caught in a consuming fire.

"Hurry," she gasped. "Rerun later."

He couldn't pass that up. All the finesse he'd been planning ceased to matter as the firestorm took over. As soon as she lay back, he slid over her, her delicious curves melding with his angles in all the best ways possible.

For an instant he couldn't even move because it felt so good. Catching her face between his hands, he looked down into her blue eyes. Botticelli angel. His for now.

Then he slid himself into her, feeling her rise up to meet him. Her legs twined around his hips, holding him as close as she could, and her body arched in response to his every thrust.

Almost too soon, she stiffened and cried out, a shudder running through her from head to foot. He couldn't contain himself another minute and joined her, erupting into her as if he were turning inside out.

When he collapsed on her, her hands settled lightly on his shoulders. A welcome. The most beautiful welcome of all.

GEORGE FINALLY HITCHED a long ride on a big rig headed in the right direction. This one had pulled up alongside him as he'd been walking down the shoulder in the dark, unwilling to risk sticking his thumb out for fear the law would take an interest.

But this guy seemed bored with his long haul and wanted someone to chat with. The radio was unusually quiet. Well, George was a good talker, able to readily make up entertaining tales, and it was a small price to pay for getting to the truck stop just outside Conard City.

He cast himself in the role of a down-on-his-luck bartender who was heading home to see his sick mother. That one always brought sympathy his way. But he didn't linger over those details, instead coming up with amusing stories about things he'd supposedly experienced while tending bar. Soon enough, the driver was chuckling, and with the laughter the guy decided he liked George. George knew how to read people, and this one was in his pocket. Now he was assured the guy wouldn't drop him off at a crossroads in the middle of nowhere.

Eventually the driver asked him about being out of work. "I thought a bartender could always get a job."

"I will eventually, after I look in on my mother. But I was stupid, man. This woman looked thirty years old at least, and I served her without asking for ID. Bitch got me canned because she was working for the state. Trying to catch ordinary joes like me."

"That stinks," the truck driver said.

"Ah, my fault," George said. "It's getting harder and harder to tell how old a person is by looking. Always check the ID."

The driver snorted. "She must have been pretty."

George laughed. "Believe it. But I was still stupid."

"I make it a rule never to pick up riders," the driver remarked. "But I picked you up. I figured, what's the harm? I dumped my load in Omaha, couldn't find a return load anywhere, so I'm driving an empty trailer and burning gas. I ain't got nothin' to steal."

"What about your truck?" George asked.

"Not likely. This baby is old. She keeps going because I hold her together. Besides, she's got LoJack. I don't get home on time, my wife will be calling the cops."

"Tight rein, huh?" George asked. "No time for a little fun on the road?"

The driver laughed again. "Not for me."

Satisfied he had the driver exactly where he wanted him, George began to consider his plans for the days ahead. This guy would leave him at the truck stop, but he had no idea where Dory was in relation to that. She might have settled into a log cabin in the middle of nowhere.

Naw, probably not, he decided. He gathered from what little he knew of her work that she must need a great internet connection. Those generally didn't reach isolated cabins.

So she'd be somewhere in or near one of the towns. There were a bunch of really small ones, then the big one where he'd be dropped off.

He rubbed his chin, feeling the beard he'd begun growing almost as soon as he'd been freed. Right now he didn't look a whole lot like himself, which was exactly what he wanted. The gray streaks in it helped, too, making him look a lot older.

But this town he was going to wasn't that big. It might be best to lie low as much as possible. Maybe people minded their own business, and maybe they didn't. He couldn't risk the latter, couldn't risk people commenting on a stranger who didn't have a job and didn't seem to be passing through. The last thing he wanted was anyone's attention.

The truck stop would probably be a reasonably safe

place to hang on and off, with a constant turnover of clientele. But apart from that?

He needed to keep low.

Which multiplied the problem of locating Dory.

Around five in the morning, he gave up his comfortable ride with the trucker, asking to be let out in a larger town, away from his destination. A town that would give him the freedom to plan and the tools he might need.

And that sign about Rodeo Days meant there'd be a lot of strangers around. Good. Not a soul would notice him unless he wanted it.

He waved goodbye to the trucker as he stood beside the road. He'd long ago learned not to do anything that might make someone remember him, so he was always polite and friendly but not too much so.

Smiling, he started to whistle. He was on his way, getting it together.

LIMP WITH PLEASURE and fatigue, Dory could hardly move. She lay on the bed waiting for Cadell to return and felt Flash lick her hand. The air was filled with the musky aroma of their lovemaking, delicious to her.

"Down," she said, barely able to muster the energy for that one word. She had forgotten that she could feel so good, so sated, so complete…if she ever had before. She felt the corners of her mouth curve, as if she couldn't stop smiling. Heck, her whole body was smiling.

She just hoped her impatience hadn't turned off Cadell. Well, she didn't know how to be a lady. She was a woman, and nothing in her life had made her feel she needed to take a backseat, although she'd learned online that there were plenty of men out there who wanted just that. Hence her secrecy about her identity.

Well, that and George. She knew he was coming. She could feel it. Somehow she would have to face him down, get him to move on and leave her alone. Money. With him it had always been about money. She'd gladly give him her last dime if he'd move to another continent.

The bed dipped as Cadell returned. She was surprised she'd delved so deeply into her thoughts that she hadn't heard him coming. The light was still dim, coming from the bathroom, but she could see he was smiling. She reached up a hand and cupped his cheek.

"I'm limp," she told him.

His smile widened. "You're not the only one. And we're not done."

Her heart leaped. "We're not?"

"Oh, no. I hardly got to explore you. That needs a bit of correction." He stretched out and propped his head on his hand, still smiling. "Close your eyes. Just *feel.*"

Excitement was already galloping through her veins, though just a minute ago she would have thought it impossible. She obliged, closing her eyes, nearly holding her breath in anticipation.

First came the featherlight touch of his fingertips, tracing the shell of her ear, the line of her jaw. Passing sweetly over her lips until they parted and she drew a long, quivering breath. With each moment, every nerve in her body felt as if it were growing more sensitive.

Then his touch trailed lower, remaining light, offering no pressure. Across her shoulders, her collarbones, down to her fingertips and then back up the inside of her arm. Now a helpless shiver raced through her.

"Easy," he murmured. "Just enjoy."

Oh, man, was she enjoying. When he found her breasts at last, she bit her lip, hoping...and his fingertips moved on. She could have cried out.

He trailed his hand down, tracing the most fragile of ribbons across her midriff, then lower, making circles around her navel, moving side to side but taking ever so long to dip lower.

Just as she thought he would, his hand slipped down her thigh, stroking the outside first, then the inside, but coming no nearer to her most sensitive places.

He was driving her out of her mind with an impatient excitement like none she had ever known. Then her other leg, down the outside then up until he returned to her belly.

Now! Please, now! Her thoughts had turned into a stew of boiling need and even some fear that he might leave her like this, hungry but unsated. She felt as if she were vibrating from head to toe, like a stringed instrument that he was playing skillfully.

Oh, so skillfully.

Then, causing her to suck air between her teeth, his fingers slid downward and found her moist cleft. She could no longer hold still but arched upward against his touch, needing so much more.

For a little while, he indulged her, stroking her with gentle fingers, but then it stopped.

She couldn't even open her eyes, she couldn't stand it. "Cadell…"

"Easy."

She felt him part her legs, felt him settle between them, then the most exquisite sensation in the world, almost painful in its intense pleasure. With his tongue, he drove her upward until she mindlessly dug her fingers into the sheets and hung on for dear life.

When at last she reached the pinnacle and shattered into a million flaming pieces, all that was left of her was woman, flying free among stars.

CADELL'S ARMS WRAPPED her in warmth and strength. He'd pulled the blanket up over them and held her close, close enough that she could feel his hard contours, the slightest movement as he breathed. The whisper of his breath on her hair. Her own arm lay over his waist, feeling more of his warmth, more of his skin.

The intimacy of the moment pierced her. She'd taken a couple of lovers before, never for more than a single night or two, but those experiences had been nothing like this. She'd walked away from both of them thinking she was really not missing much by avoiding men.

All that had changed in an earthquake named Cadell. The intimacy. The closeness. Again, the understanding floated through her. She had never felt this close to anyone, at least not since her childhood.

She should have run from it. Where had love and trust gotten her the last time? But she could not quell it. It filled her, altering her, changing her, and she didn't want to fight it.

Come what may, she thought sleepily, she was going to be a different person. Maybe a better person. Now if only they could get rid of the threat.

Then, safe in the arms of a man who had taken it on himself to protect her, she drifted off into the happiest dreams she had enjoyed for years.

CADELL AWOKE FIRST in the morning. Slipping carefully out of bed, he pulled on his jeans and boots, then took Flash for a run in the backyard. When they came back in, he started a pot of coffee for himself and began looking for something to use to make a breakfast for the two of them.

After last night, he had the appetite of a lumberjack.

Then he paused, realization setting in almost hard enough to knock the wind from him. The woman who had warned him that she didn't trust anyone had trusted *him*.

And not just last night. Little by little she'd been opening herself, sharing herself, talking about herself, her feelings, her thoughts. No longer was it all about George. No, it was sometimes about the changes in her, her personal growth.

She'd shared herself in so many ways over the last

couple of weeks. Even announced she was thinking about meeting other people.

Dory had come a long way.

And so had he. He sat abruptly, waiting for the coffee, waiting for the changes inside him to settle. He'd tried to help a woman who had good reason to be afraid. He'd thought at the outset he'd give her the dog, maybe check up on her from time to time. Instead his days had steadily become more and more entwined with hers. Especially since the moment when she had shared her graphic of the murder with him. He'd looked into a small child's heart and seen how it had affected the woman she'd become.

With that, all distance on his part had vanished. All thoughts of forever avoiding another debacle like Brenda went away. He'd crossed his own personal barriers with Dory, and he wasn't at all sure he wanted to put them back in place.

What he did know was he wanted more than a one-night stand with her. Whether it grew into anything more than casual, only time could tell, but for the first time since Brenda, he was willing to give it a chance.

Besides, he was growing very fond of Dory. As she emerged from her shell, he saw more than a Botticelli angel who took his breath away. He saw a rose blossoming into fullness, no longer a cramped bud hiding in work and her computers. She was showing strength. Fortitude. Determination. She was no longer talking of running.

For his part, he felt truly alive in every way this morning. He kind of hoped the feeling would last.

He'd rediscovered the man he used to be. What could be wrong with that? It felt good.

Smiling, he went back to trying to devise a breakfast from the slim pickings in her fridge. He guessed he was going to have to be the cook as long as they stayed together.

"I thought I smelled coffee," Dory said from the kitchen doorway. She wore a blue robe and slippers.

He looked over his shoulder and smiled at her. "It's there if you want some. I hope you don't mind, but I was looking through your fridge and cupboards trying to find something to make for breakfast."

She arched a brow at him. "You don't eat cereal?"

"Not often. Most of what you have in there is too sweet."

A slow smile spread across her face. "Try it at 3:00 a.m. after working for ten hours. It's the absolute greatest energizer." She started to move past him, but he snagged her around her waist and drew her down onto his lap. At once she wrapped her arms around his neck.

He smiled into those blue, blue eyes of hers. "Good morning, darlin'." Then he kissed her soundly, feeling his body stir in response. This, he thought dimly, was not likely to lead to breakfast.

He pulled his head back reluctantly, enjoying the way her eyes had closed, the way her mouth looked slightly swollen. Beautiful. "But this won't feed us," he said gruffly.

"Depends," she answered pertly, her eyes opening. Then with a little laugh, she slid off his lap. "You're too distracting. So no cereal, huh?"

Then she pulled a can of soup out of the cupboard. "Will you eat lunch for breakfast? Because I can make a mean grilled cheese sandwich, and with a little tomato soup, I think we can top the tanks."

Why hadn't he thought of that? Dang, was he getting too mired in his routine?

What made the breakfast wonderful, however, was the woman sitting across from him, smiling and chatting as if she hadn't a care in the world.

He knew that wouldn't last. It couldn't.

"I need to go in to work for a couple of hours today," he told her as he ate his second sandwich. "But then, if you can spare the time, we can go out to my place. Doc Windwalker is bringing me a young dog he thinks might be perfect to train as a companion for a little autistic boy."

"I thought you didn't do that kind of thing."

"I don't do it often. I can call on help if I need it, but this has landed in my lap. The family can't afford to go elsewhere, so…" He shrugged. "We'll see what we can do."

The smile she gave him then made him feel about ten feet tall.

BY THE TIME Dory showered, dressed and went to her computers, she found a raft of messages awaiting her. The team was discussing a potential new project and whether they could accomplish what the client wanted in the time allotted. Dory read the specs, such as they were, and the comments from the rest of the team. It was clear everyone wanted to do it, but it was going to be a huge challenge, something they'd never done before. Almost like going back to the very beginning of graphics design. It intrigued her, too, as she thought about it.

Then a private message popped up from Reggie.

Where you been?

Busy. Sorry. Life.

Yeah, I know about the whole life thing. Was getting worried because of your brother.

I'm fine. Pretty protected, too, by a trained guard dog. She didn't want to mention Cadell. Not their business.

Well, good. But I needed to let you know something. We had a hack attempt from a library in Nebraska a few days ago. Our webmaster didn't think a whole lot about it, just put it in his report. Anyway, I'm telling you because the hacker was trying to get into our personnel files. He failed, but...

Thanks, Dory typed back quickly, even as her heart slammed into high gear. How many days ago?

There was a pause and she could imagine Reggie switching to another file. Then came the answer.

Five days.

Five days was long enough to get here from Nebraska. Plenty long enough. All of a sudden the day didn't seem as beautiful as it had just a few minutes ago.

Then another ping. Reggie typing more.

If there's anything at all we can do, just ask. Nobody's happy about this.

Thanks, she typed again. I really appreciate it.

Now about that new project...

She was glad to think about the project. Work had been her salvation for a long time, and it was again that morning. The less room she made in her thoughts for her brother, the better she felt.

Heck, she hadn't even had a nightmare last night. That made her smile even though she felt as if a dark cloud were steadily moving her way.

But then it occurred to her that she needed to let Cadell know about this. It might be nothing. Or it might be George.

DORY'S PHONE CALL blew up Cadell's plan for the day. Or at least delayed things a bit. He called Mike Windwalker and asked him to postpone bringing the family and the dog to his place for a couple of hours. Mike thought he could manage that, but if not what about tomorrow?

"Tomorrow would be fine, too, but I'm pretty sure I can look over the situation this afternoon. I'm just sorry about the holdup."

"I know all about that," Mike responded drily. "I'm a veterinarian, remember?"

A vet with a wife and a daughter in a wheelchair. He probably hated it when he couldn't get home on time.

Then he headed for Gage's office. The sheriff looked up expectantly.

"I'm not sure this means anything," Cadell began, "but I think we need to check it out. Dory's coworker told her that someone attempted to hack the company's personnel files from a library in Nebraska."

"Maybe nothing," Gage said, but as he straightened, it was clear he didn't believe it. "Can we find out which library?"

"I'll call Dory right now."

It took Dory a few minutes to realize how many times her cell phone rang. Persistent, whoever it was. She surfaced from her study of the new program specs and reached for it. Cadell? And for once she felt as if her heart smiled.

"Hey," he said warmly. "Got a question for you."

"Sure."

"Is there any way to find out which library that hack attempt came from?"

"Hang on while I message Reggie. It might take a few if he's busy. Would it be better if I called you back?"

"I'll wait." There was no mistaking the resolve in Cadell's voice. The hack attempt, which she had been trying so hard to forget, surged back to the foreground, and with it her level of anxiety. Clearly Cadell didn't think it was innocent.

"God, what next," she muttered as she typed rapidly to Reggie.

Cadell answered her. "Next I'm going to come over and get you, and we're going to meet a family with an autistic child and try to make him happy. In the meantime…"

In the meantime. Yeah. She drummed her fingers impatiently, waiting for Reggie. When nearly five minutes had passed, she got his familiar Yo.

I need to know which library that hack attempt came from.

What I got is an IP.

Give it to me, I'll look it up.

K.

Another pause, then a string of numbers, three at a time with a decimal between them.

Thanks, she typed. I'm liking the project, btw.

Great!

Then she picked up her cell. "I've got the IP address. For nongeeks, that means it can lead you right to the computer that was used, as long as he didn't use an anonymous server."

"I'll take it."

"I can also look it up for you."

He gave a quiet laugh. "Maybe you should do that. We could use a more advanced IT department here, but who has the funds?"

"I hear a lot of police departments have that problem and hence still use fax machines."

"You'd be right."

"So last century," she remarked, trying to sound light when she didn't feel good about this at all. It could be a random hacker, though. It always amazed her how many brains wasted themselves on trying to disrupt other people's computers just for kicks.

It didn't take long to trace the IP. The internet was decent about keeping track of itself, or it would have blown up and become useless from the start. "Okay," she said to Cadell. "It's one of four computers assigned to a library in Landoun, Nebraska. Small, like Conard City."

"So maybe the librarian will remember someone. Okay, thanks. I'll get back to you shortly."

She wondered if she would survive waiting even a few minutes. Then, with determination, she pushed all thoughts of George aside. Focus on her job. She was good at burying everything else.

Soon she was lost in a world of storyboards the team had begun to build, offering a few opinions, making some changes that would be a little less difficult to carry out.

But then her phone rang, and all hope of distraction fled. It was Cadell.

"Okay," he said. "The librarian didn't recognize George's inmate photo when we emailed it to her. But she did say a few days ago a man she didn't know used the computer for several hours. He had a thick beard, though. So I'm sending George's inmate photo to the state to have them put a beard on it. Just in case. I'll pass it by the librarian and see if we come up with someone who resembles her unknown man."

Dory sagged in her chair. "Thank you," she answered. "I have the software to put a beard on him, too, if it would save time." She needed to know. Even as she sagged, a vise had gripped her heart. She was sure it was George. Who else would be trying to penetrate Animation's personnel files?

"Dory? You know this is slim."

"Then why am I having so much trouble believing it?" she snapped.

He paused. "So you've got software that can do this? I'll be right over with his faxed photo."

She disconnected, staring at her screen, knowing full well that she wasn't going to be able to focus until she'd dealt with the photograph. It was as if everything had moved out of the realm of possibility and into the realm of reality.

She felt a poke on her leg and saw Flash nudging her and looking up at her. Almost automatically she reached out to pet him. "Can you hold it until Cadell gets here?"

Because all of sudden she didn't even want to walk into her backyard alone.

GEORGE HEISTED A pickup and switched the plates with a similar vehicle before pulling it out of the dirt parking lot from among a great many others. Rodeo Days must be a big thing around here. Once he was safely out of town, he hit the state highway, and at the first opportunity in the middle of nowhere, he pulled onto the shoulder and began to check what was in the truck. Registration and insurance. Good, but he still had no license. He'd better not get stopped.

And a gun? That might be useful. Although guns made a mess, and he wanted Dory's death to look accidental. In the back of the truck, which was dirty enough to convince him it was used for some serious work, he found other items that could be useful, from rope to barbed wire, regular tools and then something he couldn't at first identify.

Curious, he pulled out the three-foot-long rod by its handle, then noticed the two tines on the end. It looked like a Taser. An awfully big Taser. He pressed the button and saw the spark with satisfaction. A cattle prod. He smiled. That could be useful. He just wished it were smaller in size so it could be more easily hidden.

He climbed back into the cab and drove toward Conard City. Not much longer now. He had plenty of tools in this truck that could be useful. Now all he had to do was find his sister without being seen himself.

There was a battered, misshapen cowboy hat on the seat beside him, looking like someone's castoff. He put it on, pulling it low over his brow. Beard or no beard, the less anyone could see of his face, the better. He whistled tunelessly, thinking that it was a beautiful day. The wide-open spaces didn't even bother him as much anymore.

Life was finally going his way.

Chapter Twelve

The photo Cadell brought Dory was from a fax machine. Not the highest resolution, but she put it through her scanner and some software to enhance the clarity. Then she plugged it into the software that would add a beard.

"Did the librarian say what kind of beard?"

"Full. Not terribly long."

"Okay. This is going to take a while, though."

"How long do you think?"

"A few hours."

"Then let's go see an autistic child about a dog."

"Sounds good to me." The last thing she wanted to do was hang around here wondering and worrying. Keeping busy had always been her salvation. But then she found she couldn't stand up.

"Oh, God," she whispered.

"What?"

"I just looked at my brother for the first time in a quarter century. He could be a stranger, Cadell. I barely recognize him."

"Let's hope he has the same problem with you." He squatted. "You going to be all right?"

"I always am," she said irritably. But her legs still felt like noodles, and she reached for the fax again, staring at a face that had changed an awful lot but still belonged to the brother she had once loved.

"It's a shame," she said presently.

"What is?"

"That he was never the person I thought he was. That person could have done wonderful things with his life. Instead…" She didn't finish. She tossed the photo to one side.

He straightened and touched her shoulder. "Put George on the back burner while your software works. And remember, if he really is looking for you, he has to find you first."

"Maybe I need a wig and some big sunglasses."

He looked at her, then his eyes twinkled.

On the ride out to Cadell's place, she once again drank in the countryside. At first it had been so different from anything she'd known before that it had looked dry and scrubby to her, not especially attractive except for the mountains.

But time had taught her to see differently. All that space, dotted occasionally with copses of trees, a lot of scrub and the tumbleweeds, fascinated her. She loved to see the wind catch a tumbleweed and carry it along.

"Every place has its charms," she remarked. "It took me a while to see them here."

Cadell tossed her a grin before returning his attention to the roads. "I was overwhelmed when I first moved to Seattle. All the green seemed suffocating—there were no long lines of sight. Kinda claustrophobic at first. But it didn't take long before I began to see it differently. Anyway, when I came home here to visit, *this* place looked bad to me. I used to run up into the mountains just to see the forest. So yeah, I get what you mean."

"Well, I'm beginning to appreciate it. Mostly I love the mountains, though."

"One of these days soon I'll take you up there. Some great vistas overlooking the valley. And lots of trees."

She laughed, feeling the last remnants of her concern about George slip away. He could wait, at least for a few hours. Being with Cadell was more important.

And certainly a whole lot more pleasant.

CADELL HAD JUST enough time to make some coffee to offer to Mike when the vet arrived in his fully equipped van. The man had to be ready at a moment's notice to provide care to livestock almost anywhere around here, and he had half a clinic in the back of his vehicle.

A tall Cheyenne with black hair he refused to cut short, Mike was a great guy. Over the last couple of years his practice had grown by leaps and bounds. So had his kennels and the number of dogs and cats he had for adoption.

He greeted Cadell warmly, asking after the ostriches.

"Itsy and Bitsy are doing fine, as far as I can tell."

"Itsy and Bitsy?" Mike's eyes widened.

"Blame her," Cadell said with a grin, indicating Dory with his thumb. Then he introduced the two of them. "So now, what kind of dog did you bring me?"

"A good one, I think," Mike said, walking around

to the back of the van. "He's a mutt, already neutered. Near as I can tell he's got some golden Lab in him and something much smaller. Regardless, he's just about two, so he's lost some of the puppy energy, he's smart and he listens. So we'll see."

Mike opened the carrier in the back of his van, grabbed a lead already attached to the dog's collar, then let the animal jump down.

Cadell thought he looked like a somewhat miniaturized golden Lab, good-looking but probably not big enough to intimidate a child of about six. "Great choice," he said. "Listen, you know where the coffee is. Go on in and help yourself. I want to run him around the corral and get to know him. Does he have a name?"

"I've been trying to avoid that."

Cadell arched a brow. "So what have you been calling him?"

"Dog."

"Ha!" Cadell laughed, and Dory joined in.

"But why avoid a name?" she asked Mike.

"Because I'll get attached. Because whoever adopts my animals is going to want to name them. I realize that's ridiculous, because I've found you can change a dog's name a dozen times and he'll still answer. But..." He shrugged. "Okay, I don't want to get attached. Sooner or later I've got to let them go."

At that moment, Flash, who'd been allowed his freedom in the kennels and fenced yard, came dashing up to sit beside Dory. He regarded the new dog inquisitively, tilting his head a little to one side, his tail sweeping the ground in a friendly manner.

"Test one," remarked Cadell. The small golden came trotting over and began to sniff Flash from top to bottom. Flash lay down as if to make it easier, and soon the golden was lying right beside him. Friends, it seemed.

"Okay, no dog aggression," remarked Cadell. "Dory, keep Flash beside you while I take Dog into the corral."

DORY NOTICED AS she and Mike walked to the back of the house that the ostriches leaned over their pen's fence as if they wanted a better look.

"I don't think they've forgotten me," Mike remarked. "Or the injections I gave them. I'm not a popular person with them."

"Is anyone?" Dory asked.

Mike chuckled. "They're really not so bad, usually. They'd rather run than fight. But getting into a fight with one...well, I wouldn't recommend it. They may not have teeth, but they can peck with a lot of force. Then, while the nail on their single clawed toe on each foot isn't the sharpest, they pack a hell of a kick. Bones could break. If they're trapped and feel threatened, a human might not survive it."

Good to know, Dory thought. Not that she ever intended to get into the pen with them.

Cadell was already at work with Dog, and from his face and posture, Dory thought he was pleased. In almost no time at all, the dog was following commands to sit and stay. When Cadell saw Mike and Dory approach the corral fence, he called out, "Good one. Smart and eager to please. That's what we want, right? A companion."

"As far as I know, they don't have any other needs for their son. Just that he be perfectly safe with the animal because…well, I guess the child can get rough and loud sometimes."

"What child can't?" Cadell asked rhetorically. Then he turned his head. "I guess that's them."

Dory peered in the direction he was looking and saw a dust cloud just beginning to come up the long drive.

Soon a family of three, one of whom was a thin boy of about six, were coming around the house to the back. The boy was incredibly silent, Dory thought. Sadly so. He walked past the kennels of dogs, looking at them but not making a sound.

His parents were young, dressed like a hardworking ranch couple, in jeans and somewhat faded shirts. Neither of them held the boy's hand.

"Brad doesn't like to be touched," the woman said. "I'm Letty Embrow, and this is my husband, Jase." She looked at Mike. "What do you think?"

"I picked the one I think is best. Cadell's pleased with him."

Her eyes trailed to Cadell. She seemed like a pleasant woman, but right now there was a deep tension riding her. Because she didn't know how her son was going to react? Or was she afraid the dog might do something?

They walked together, with the Embrows in the rear, until they reached the gate into the training yard. Cadell looked at the parents. "Can I talk to him, or do you need to do that?"

"Let's see what happens," Letty answered.

So Cadell squatted and looked at the child from about five feet away. "I hear you want a dog."

Dory thought the boy's gaze fixated for the first time since he'd arrived. His attention was fastened to Cadell.

"I have one I think you'll like, Brad. But you and I have to go inside the fence to meet him. If you like him, I'll get him ready to go home with you."

Cadell glanced up. "I may need a couple of days to be sure he's well trained, but I'd like you to bring Brad every afternoon to work with him. Doable?"

Both parents nodded, and Cadell returned his attention to the boy. "Want to come through the fence and meet the dog, Brad?"

For the first time, the boy became animated. He bobbed his head in the affirmative. Dog was waiting on the other side of the fence a few feet away. The instant Cadell opened it wide enough, the little boy slipped through and ran right up to the dog.

Dory heard everyone's breath catch. Then Brad threw his arms around Dog's neck and crowed, "Doggy! Doggy!"

And Dog didn't seem to mind it one bit.

Magic, thought Dory. There was still magic in the world.

THE LONG SUMMER twilight covered the world when Cadell and Dory got back to her house. They'd taken time to care for the animals, cleaning kennels, letting the ostriches into the larger corral so they could clean up their small pen, then putting them back in the pen and feeding them again.

They stopped at Maude's on the way back for carry-out, because Dory was concerned about her work. "I keep taking time off," she told Cadell frankly. "I've got to make up for at least some of it."

"Yeah, for me working with the canines is the largest part of my job. I appreciate all your help, though."

"I've enjoyed doing it. I never really had the chance to find out before, but I like animals. Someday I want to meet the goats."

"That's easy enough."

They pulled into the driveway behind her car, then climbed out with the bags and started for the front door.

The evening suddenly changed for Dory. "God," she whispered.

Cadell stopped and faced her. "What?"

"I feel watched. That's ridiculous." She tried to brush it away, but the feeling was an icy one, just awful.

Cadell set the bags on the rickety porch bench. "Unlock the door, but stay here. I'm going to make sure no one got into your house."

"Why would…"

"I'm just going to make sure. Meanwhile, you look

around and see if something has changed right around the house, something minor that troubled you, okay?"

So she stood there with Flash sitting at her side. Foolish as it felt, the feeling would not go away, and she put him on guard. The dog missed little, but when she ordered Flash to guard her, his attention grew more intense.

She studied the house as Cadell had told her to but didn't see anything amiss. Not that she'd paid that much attention. The house had never been intended to be more than a way station for her.

Although maybe... But she pushed the thought aside. She and Cadell might be having sex now, but that didn't necessarily mean anything about next week.

She watched as lights turned on inside the house. He was going room by room. Like someone could hide in her very few rooms. She might have been amused if the itchy feeling of being watched hadn't persisted.

She studied the street, looking for another human being, but most humans were probably indoors eating dinner, or maybe in their backyards having a picnic. The street was as silent as it was empty.

She heard an engine start way down toward the edge of town. A battered old red pickup appeared eventually, and she watched it approach. Before it got near, however, Cadell opened the door.

"All clear inside. Did you note anything?"

"Nope." She stepped in beside him, hardly noticing as the pickup rolled by behind her. "I guess I was just feeling too good most of the day. God forbid I should forget George for too long."

His eyes crinkled as he smiled, but she didn't miss the way he locked the door behind them.

"Do you want to check your computer for the image of that guy first, or do you want to eat? I'd hate for the food to get cold. Maude's a master with steak."

"Let's eat." Honestly, right now she didn't want to see her brother's face again, bearded or not.

Cadell carried the bags into the kitchen. Flash followed along hopefully, but he got dry food and a fresh bowl of water. Dory wondered what Cadell would think if she fed the dog people food. Sometimes she was tempted.

They sat facing each other, Cadell with a tall coffee from Maude's, she with another one of her inevitable soft drinks. The sandwiches were perfect, the steak tender enough to melt in the mouth, and still warm. He'd been right not to wait.

"I'm surprised you didn't dismiss my feeling," she said when her appetite settled into more reasonable proportions. She had no idea what had made her so hungry. Must have been all that fresh air, because it wasn't unusual for her to miss lunch.

"I never discount the feeling of being watched. Plenty of people get it sometimes, and the amazing thing is that plenty of people are right. It's not always important, of course, but when you're a cop and you get the feeling someone is focused on you? You don't ignore it."

"I just want you to know I appreciated it. It's not a sensation I've had very often. Besides, there was no reason to be afraid of it with you right there."

Again that smile danced in his dark eyes. "I'm no superhero, but thanks for the vote of confidence."

He really was a nice guy, she thought as she continued eating. She'd have grown impatient with herself long ago. Amorphous fears about a brother who might never want to see her again. She wished she could just erase him from her memory.

But erasure had proved impossible, and Cadell wasn't about to dismiss the possibility that George might feel he had business with her. Money business. Well, that wouldn't surprise her.

She shifted a little in her chair. "Do you have any idea how much I inherited?"

He swallowed and took a drink of coffee. "Not really. The news articles from back then suggested a million-dollar insurance policy."

She snorted. "So much more sensational, huh? No, actually it was about half of that, including what my godparents got for me from the sale of the house. That's a lot of money—it might have grown over the years sitting in CDs and bank accounts, but I don't know. You see, I have a vice."

His brows rose. "Tell me it's not cocaine."

If she'd felt more comfortable, she would have laughed. "No. I can't touch it, I told you. But when I turned twenty-one I made just one change to the trust with my godparents' permission… I started donating half the interest."

"That's a *vice*?"

She shrugged faintly. "Some financial advisers think so, but not me. They handle the trust and apparently keep it growing. Anyway, the interest goes to various causes, mostly those helping children. Which brings me around to today. Brad couldn't have afforded a companion dog without you and Mike Windwalker stepping up, right?"

"I don't believe so."

She nodded. "Maybe that'll be my next charity. Kids like Brad who need companion animals. They shouldn't be out of anyone's reach."

A warm smile spread across his face. "I like the way you think, Dory Lake."

"George wouldn't agree. When my godparents set up the trust they made it clear that they wanted me to save it for the future. I didn't have any reason to disagree, but when I turned twenty-one, ownership passed to me. I left everything the way they'd made it except the use of the interest. And that's when I made it irrevocable. If George had ever tried to contact me for money, I wouldn't have responded. Not by then."

"Theoretically he didn't know where you were to contact you."

"Probably not. My godparents moved a lot because of Uncle Bill's job." She sighed and pushed her dinner to one side. "I'm tired of every discussion coming back to him. I want him gone. Out of my life. Not constantly hanging over my head." She closed her eyes briefly, then opened them so she could see his face. "The thing is, I think I create that threat myself more than anything. He might be headed to the opposite end of the country. He might not want to see me any more than I want to see him."

"It's possible."

She didn't miss the doubt in his tone. He believed George was going to show up. Her biggest fear was going to materialize. And Cadell intended to be at her side as much as he could. Gratitude filled her.

She looked down at Flash. "He'll take care of George."

"He'll certainly try."

The word hovered in the air along with her fears. Flash would try. No guarantees.

"Will you stay tonight?" she asked, trying to sound casual.

"I wouldn't be anywhere else in the world."

GEORGE NEVER WOULD have dreamed it would finally be so easy to find his sister. Changing license plates on the truck had made him think of something that hadn't occurred to him before: she had a car, and that was information he could get for a fee from a private company online. The library in the place he thought of as "Rodeo Town" along with a prepaid debit card, had made it possible for him to find out what kind of vehicle she was driving. It still bore Kansas plates, the site claimed, which would stick out in Wyoming, even though the site wouldn't give him the plate number or VIN.

And lo and behold, when he drove through Conard City late last night, he'd seen it. There she was. The only problem was that parked behind her car was a police SUV. Sheriff's department. K-9 Unit blazoned on its side.

Curious, he'd parked up the street and waited until it was evident that cop wasn't going anywhere else.

Hell. She'd hooked up with a guy—fast work, he thought—and worse, she'd hooked up with a cop. A freaking cop.

Anger shook him to his core, and he cleared out of town before he blew his stack. Pounding on a steering wheel and cussing loudly would only have drawn unwanted attention.

It wasn't long, though, before he regained his self-control and came back to town. Rage was a tool to be used, not something he should ever let control him. He knew that.

He kept watch from a safe distance. And what he'd seen had both given him ideas and frustrated him more.

The cop never left her side. When they came out of her house in the late morning, it was together and with a dog. Probably the cop's K-9, although he had to wonder why Dory was holding the leash.

He also had to admire his sister. She'd been a cute kid, everyone said so, but she'd grown into a stunning woman. Too bad he had to get rid of her. If he'd thought he could have talked her into working with him, she'd have been a great asset. But from everything he could tell about her—which wasn't a whole lot—she had chosen to live on the right side of the law.

What a waste.

He watched them drive out of town toward the mountains and hung a safe distance back. If he lost them…well, there was always tomorrow.

He trailed behind, but not so far he didn't see them turn in to a ranch. He kept going for another couple of miles and then headed back. In the distance, near a two-story white house, the cop's vehicle was still parked. It must be his place.

Ideas were beginning to swim again. Once he was sure the two of them were safely tucked in for the night at her place, he was going to come back out here and see what kind of opportunity he could create.

Because opportunities were always there, just waiting for a clear enough eye to see them.

He'd waited a long time to put an end to Dory and get what he truly deserved. He could wait a little longer.

"I'VE GOT WORK in the morning," Cadell told her later that night. Lovemaking had once again left her feeling limp and good all over. She wondered if she had been missing something all these years or if she had been missing Cadell.

She rolled lazily toward him. "No one's ever made me feel this wonderful."

He turned his head on the pillow and gave her a smile. "Now that's a great thing to hear."

"Truth."

He stirred until he was on his side, too, and draped his arm over her waist. He lifted it briefly to brush a strand of her blond hair back from her face. "Truth," he agreed. "You make me feel wonderful, too."

She sighed happily and buried her face in his shoulder.

"Work in the morning," he said again.

"I heard," she mumbled.

"Are you going to be okay?"

"I've got my work, too."

"You know I wasn't referring to that."

She did, but she didn't want to think about it. "Let's not ruin this by thinking about tomorrow. If I get uneasy, I'll run over to Betty's, okay? But don't forget, I have Flash. I wouldn't want to argue with him."

"He *does* have a lot of teeth," Cadell said, allowing the mood to lighten.

But she felt the concern in him and knew he was right. Until George was dealt with somehow, there *was* a threat. She sought a way to reassure him. "You know, I'm not exactly in the middle of nowhere. It'll be daytime, people are around, I'll have Flash, and if I scream for help, I think someone will call for it."

"You're right," he admitted. "Everyone around here would call for help and probably come running, too."

"So I'll be fine. But if you're worried about it, I'll go to Betty's."

After a moment he shook his head. "You have to work, too."

"What are you doing?"

"I've got patrol duty. I don't just train the dogs, you know." He tightened his hold on her, and she snuggled closer. "Four hours. I'll be back in four hours."

"Okay." But she didn't feel okay. Long after she felt his breathing deepen and steady, she stared into the dark and shared her mind and heart with a little girl who was still traumatized.

She doubted any number of years would entirely get her past that. It was better now, much better, even if George's release had awakened long-buried fears. But that little girl? Sometimes she needed attention, too.

BEFORE CADELL LEFT in the morning, he suggested she drive out to his place. He could meet her there shortly after noon, but he needed to check on the animals again. Maybe work with them some.

She was happy to agree. Plenty of time to work, a nice afternoon break, and then some more work this evening. Or something else, she thought with a private smile. Something else with Cadell had become the high point of her days.

Maybe a dangerous place to go, but she was going anyway. It kept hitting her that life as a hermit might provide safety, but it sure hadn't given her a lot of good times. Not good times like Cadell gave her. However long it lasted, she wanted as much as he'd give her.

She spent a little time with her eyes closed, remembering last night, remembering Cadell's smile, thinking about the way he looked striding around his ranch. Incredibly male, yet incredibly kind. She wasn't used to men who were so kind. Heck, she worked with kind men, but she didn't allow them to know she was a woman. Women weren't welcome in the men's world of computers. Although maybe she wasn't being fair to the guys she worked with.

Then she laughed. For all she knew, some of them might be women, too.

Sometime later as she was finishing up her work, she ran into a mental hitch and couldn't quite get her finger on it. Something was wrong.

Sighing, she heard an answering sigh and looked over to see Flash, his head on the floor, looking up at her as if to say, "Have you forgotten I need exercise?"

"Okay," she said. "We'll go for a run." It would clear her head about work and allow her a good excuse to let her mind wander over Cadell and all his attractive attributes. He made her body sing, true. But he was bringing long-cold parts of her back to warmth and light.

It was probably going to hurt, but right now she didn't care. She was willing to take whatever this slice of life offered her and pay the cost later.

She knew all about costs. And she knew she could survive them.

GEORGE WATCHED HER come out of the house with that dog of hers. He'd learned a little about her boyfriend last night when he'd explored the guy's ranch. Dog trainer? K-9s? Cop dogs? He looked at the dog trotting beside Dory on a leash and suspected it had been trained by that man. An extra wrinkle, but one he could deal with.

What he'd found at the ranch was the perfect way to get rid of Dory and keep himself out of it. Ostriches had a kick worse than a boxer's punch. All he had to do was get Dory in with them and then stir them up. That'd look like an accident, especially since he planned to break the lock on the pen when it was over. At worst it would look like she'd been trying to round them up after the lock failed.

But nobody would think they'd been used as a murder weapon. And thanks to the electric fencing, she wouldn't be able to climb out.

Man, sometimes his own brilliance blinded him.

CADELL SPENT HIS morning missing Dory. Not a good sign. He'd vowed a long time ago not to get into another deep relationship, and here he was violating his own oath. Dory wasn't the best bet, either. He doubted she fully trusted him, and that meant he'd be wise not to trust her completely, either.

Nor could he be sure she wouldn't just pack up and leave. She'd been avoiding real human contact for a long time and had said as much. She preferred being a hermit. This was an interlude for her, a bit of entertainment by helping him with his dogs, a change of pace. But soon she'd probably feel it was interfering with her work, and she'd want to crawl back into her safe emotional cave. Especially if they couldn't somehow put the issue of George to rest for good.

He sighed and prowled the roads, filling in for Carter Birch, whose wife had just had a baby. He hated patrolling. Yeah, he'd done thousands of miles of it over the years, but back in Seattle at least he was likely to see something or do something, even if it was only writing a traffic ticket. Out here on the prairie and the foot of the mountains, there was almost nothing to do unless he got a call.

It was important, of course. If a call came, the idea was that a patrol wouldn't be too far away. Distance could cost a life in an emergency. But he vastly preferred training the dogs and K-9 officers, and he often wondered just how he could expand his business so it would become full-time.

Again his thoughts trailed back to Dory, and he glanced at his watch. Another hour, then he could start heading toward his place to meet her. Another hour.

He pulled over to the side of the road and poured himself a cup of coffee from the thermos bottle he'd had Maude fill for him that morning. Still hot, still good.

He scanned the wide-open spaces that led up the mountains. A beautiful summer day easing slowly into autumn. The air was dry, the breeze steady.

And he wished he could ignore the sense that Dory needed him. She was fine. She had Flash, she was at work, she'd have called if she needed help and the department would have called him.

Everything was fine.

So why couldn't he believe it?

Chapter Thirteen

Dory figured she could give Flash a good thirty-minute run before she'd need to shower and head out to Cadell's ranch. She was eagerly looking forward to seeing him again, and not all her good reasons for avoiding those feelings would get rid of that.

Oh, well, she thought as she ran down the sidewalk, her jogging shoes slapping on pavement. She passed a couple in their front yard, and they exchanged waves and smiles. Maybe getting out of her shell wasn't so bad.

Her run took her to the edge of town, where a vacant lot with a brook running through it covered several acres. Tall trees grew there, and she loved the way they dappled the light. No houses were nearby, but that was okay. She had Flash.

When she reached the end of the trees, she sometimes paused to watch the brook, but today she didn't have time. "No stops today, Flash," she told him. He didn't appear to mind. Tongue lolling, he was galloping along happily at her side.

A truck pulled up, and she barely spared it a glance until a voice called to her, chilling her to her bones.

"Dory? Get in."

Turning, ice running through her veins, she saw a gun pointed at her. Then she saw the man behind it, leaning out of a battered red truck. George. *Oh, my God, George.*

"Make that dog behave or he gets the first bullet."

Neck stiff, she looked down at Flash. He was at full attention, his gaze fixed on George and the gun. Cadell had said he would recognize a threat when he saw it.

"I'm warning you, Dory. You think I won't kill that dog?"

She never doubted it. But there was only one way to take Flash off guard. Shoving her hand into her pocket, she pulled out a tennis ball.

His entire demeanor changed. His tail wagged, and for an instant she thought he was going to get down and gnaw the ball. But instead he dropped it and lowered his head as he stared at George.

"Okay, then," George said. "Bring him a few steps closer."

"No."

"I won't shoot him unless you don't do what I say. Get him closer."

Step by agonizing step, she approached, feeling Flash start to pull at the leash. He wanted to go after George.

But when they stood a few feet away, the barrel of that gun still leveled at her, George thrust the truck door open and stuck out a yellow pole. What the…

Then she heard the sizzle and Flash's yelp. He fell to the ground, jerking.

"More than one way to deal with you and that dog. Now get your behind into this truck."

She dropped the leash, looking down at Flash, relieved to see he was still breathing. It was the last relief she was able to feel.

Then, almost numb, past fear, she climbed into the passenger side of the truck. He kept the pistol aimed at her every second.

"I'll give you money," she said stiffly as he shoved the truck into gear.

"You bet your sweet butt you will. Now shut up or I'll use that prod on you."

CADELL GOT A radio call just before he was scheduled to get off duty. It was the sheriff, Gage Dalton.

"We've got Dory Lake's dog here. He's fine, but Dory's missing. Not at her house. I've put out a county-wide alert."

Just as Gage finished speaking, the alert popped up on Cadell's mobile unit, along with the rendered photo of a bearded George Lake.

Cadell jammed on the brakes, closed his eyes and gripped the steering wheel so hard his hands cramped. He didn't need to know the odds against finding someone in all these hundreds of square miles of open space.

"We're doing a door to door," Gage said. "Meantime, we've started the phone tree with the ranches. Get yourself home, Cadell."

"Home? What the hell can I do there?"

"Get us a bunch of search dogs."

THE OLD PICKUP rattled down roads that Dory recognized. A smidgen of hope awoke in her. Either she'd be able to talk her brother into taking money, or she'd find another way to deal with him. Because when they turned in to Cadell's ranch, it was well-known territory to her. She guessed that Cadell would be there in about an hour, as he'd planned…as long as the job didn't delay him. But she refused to consider that possibility. He'd come and he'd come on time. She just had to make it for one hour. Surely she could do that.

"I never did anything to you," she said trying to make herself sound small, almost childlike.

"You should have stayed in bed."

"I wish I had." She closed her eyes briefly. "I wish I'd never seen. But I never did anything to *you*."

"You took away my escape time. You ran screaming out onto the street. I thought you loved me."

"I did."

"Then why did you run, Dory. Why?"

She shook her head a little, watching Cadell's house grow closer. Soon she could see the ostriches. Dog pens out back. If she could manage to let the dogs out somehow…

Why was he bringing her here, of all places?

"I ran because I was terrified. George… I didn't even understand what I was seeing! For more than a year I could only speak two words, *red paint*. That's all I could compare it to."

He said nothing more. She struggled to think about how she could distract him. Thought of Flash and hoped he would be okay, because her poor dog hadn't done anything to deserve that shock.

And mile by mile, she had felt her fear of George transforming into hatred. Then she remembered what Cadell had said about George being her only heir.

Her heart slammed, and she realized for absolute certain, all the way to her very core, that she was not going to survive this. Far from weakening her, the knowledge pumped strength into her. If she was going to die, she wasn't going to make it easy.

"You know," she said, watching the house grow closer, "I didn't take the inheritance away from you. The court did. You can have it all if you want. I'll turn it over to you." A lie, but he wouldn't know that.

"A little late, don't you think? Twenty-five years in prison. I need to even the score more than that. Anyway, my lawyer told me that it's in a trust you can't break. You couldn't pay me enough to leave you alone now."

Her hands clenched. "I didn't put you in prison, George. I didn't testify. Hell, I couldn't even tell anyone what had happened. Conversion disorder, they called it. For more than a year I only spoke two words, and for over three months I was blind."

That caught his attention as the house rolled closer. "Blind, huh?"

"Blind," she said. "I didn't even understand what had happened. I couldn't. I had nightmares, though. Plenty of nightmares."

"You should have stayed in bed," he said again. But this time his voice was stony cold. Whatever charm he exerted on the rest of the world, he wasn't going to waste any on her. Not anymore.

They pulled up to one side of the house. The familiarity of the scene jarred Dory, contrasting as it did with George's abduction of her. This was a place where she'd always found peace and welcome. Just having George here seemed to shatter all that.

"Dory."

Reluctantly she looked at her brother. The gun was pointing at her again.

"Get out."

"Just shoot me here." Yeah, the anger was growing huge, and a mental voice warned her to rein it in. Now was not the time to stop thinking. But oh, the things she wanted to do to George right now would get her thrown in prison herself. Flash popped into her mind's eye, and a little crack broke through the anger. Her beloved Flash. This man had taken everything from her. Her parents. Her childhood. Her trust. Now even her dog.

Oh, yeah, she wanted him to pay. He hadn't paid nearly enough.

But she had to be smart, await her chance. Right now all she'd get for her efforts was a gunshot wound. So she climbed out of the truck, scanning the area, looking for anything she could use.

Curious, the ostriches watched them with those inscrutable dark eyes, but they had backed up in their pen, getting as far away as they could, unlike when Cadell showed up.

"Ostriches seem like a weird thing to have out here," George remarked.

Dory didn't answer, still trying to figure out what she could do. If she ran toward the kennels to let the dogs out, he'd probably put a bullet in her back before she got halfway around the house.

"I like those birds," her brother continued conversationally. "Big, beautiful and scaredy-cats."

She glanced at him, wondering how he could know that. But clearly he'd been out here before. When? Last night?

He motioned with the gun. "Let's go get a closer look at those birds. I hear their feathers are worth a fortune."

Was he going to kill the birds and steal their feathers? But then she realized he was still carrying that long yellow stick, the one that had zapped Flash. What the hell was he up to?

As they drew closer to the cage, the birds pulled back to the farthest side, then hunkered down, making themselves as small as possible. They didn't seem to like the strangers. Or at least George.

"That's how they protect themselves," George remarked. "They either try to become invisible or they run. Did you know they can run nearly forty miles an hour? Only a cheetah can catch one."

She wondered why the hell he was talking about this and taking her ever closer to the pen. Maybe he had gone crazy. This was making no sense.

"Now here's the deal," George said when they

reached the pen, watched by suspicious birds. "You can either go into that pen with them, or I'll zap you with this prod and put you in there myself."

Dory's heart nearly stopped. For a few seconds, her anger drained completely, leaving her filled with terror. Her knees weakened, and the urge to run nearly overwhelmed her. A sane voice in her head shouted it would do no good to run. She needed to buy time. She stiffened inwardly, feeling a crazy rush of strength. One thing became clear to her: if she was going to be in the pen with those birds, she didn't want to be paralyzed for even a few minutes. No way.

She couldn't scale the wire fence because it was electrified at the top, but maybe she could soothe the birds, keep them from getting too agitated. Just become small and inoffensive, she told herself. Maybe they'd leave her alone.

Her mouth turned dry, but she ignored it. Her hands moistened, making it difficult to work the latch. The birds remained hunkered down, watching.

And all the while, she wondered at the point of this. Was he going to shoot her inside the pen with the birds? What good would that do? Why not just leave her corpse somewhere along the roadside?

Eventually, with fumbling fingers, she opened the latch. The gate dragged on the ground as she pulled it open then slid inside, moving very slowly. Behind her, she heard George latch it once again. Then she heard an unmistakable *snick*. He'd added a padlock. From inside this pen, she didn't think it was possible to open the other gate into the corral. Whenever Cadell did it, he opened it with a mechanism on the outside.

She was breathing too heavily, in danger of becoming light-headed. She couldn't afford to faint again. Not now. So far the birds had offered no protest at her presence but stayed hunkered down.

Maybe she should imitate them. Slowly, she lowered herself to the ground, wrapping her arms around her knees.

"What do you want, George?" she asked, keeping her voice steady, beginning to hope that the birds would remain calm. God, she knew how huge they were, and she didn't like being in here with them, with those enormous feet. They didn't have talons like ordinary birds, but they each had one toe that grew a nail so large it looked like a weapon.

Anger toward George was surging again, erasing her fear, making her scan the enclosure for just one item she could use to get out of here, or to attack George once he'd finished enjoying torturing her.

The birds, though. She just couldn't figure out why he wanted her in here with the birds.

Then he told her. "I left out one interesting fact about these birds, dear sister. They have a powerful kick. If they can't run and feel threatened, they kick with enough power to break bones."

She caught her breath. If anyone could think of something like this…her brother had. But how could he make that happen?

And then she saw. Walking around the pen, he

poked his rod through the wire, and she heard the snap and sizzle. One of the birds screamed and rose to its full height.

For the first time, anger began to give way to despair. Those birds had nowhere to run. If he kept torturing them...

She closed her eyes. Cadell should be here soon, she thought. The only question was whether he'd arrive before she was kicked to death by frantic, tortured ostriches. She desperately hoped nothing would delay him.

CADELL RACED SO fast over the back roads that when he hit a rut, he literally went airborne, killing the suspension. He didn't care. As long as he didn't break an axle.

Dory was missing. Her worst nightmare had come true. Only now did he realize it was his own worst nightmare, as well.

He keyed his radio. "Nobody saw a thing?"

"Not a thing," answered Gage. "One of Jake's city cops saw the dog trailing its leash back toward her house. He recognized Flash immediately. That's all we know."

There was hope in that, Cadell tried to tell himself. At least George hadn't killed the dog. Maybe all he wanted from Dory was money, after all.

He wished he believed it.

Dasher whimpered from the backseat, voicing a protest at the rough ride. Cadell couldn't bring himself to slow down. The dog would be fine. His crate was belted in and not so big that that he was being thrown all over the back.

He pounded his fist against the steering wheel. How in hell were they going to find one woman who could be anywhere in these vast, open spaces? Hope a ranch hand came upon her before it was too late? Even with the phone tree operating, there was no way the folks on these huge ranches could check every acre. They'd have to catch sight of something by sheer chance.

No, all the phone tree would do was serve notice to be watching for anything unusual. Better than nothing, but not by much.

Then he heard the *whop* of helicopter blades pass over. So they'd taken to the air, as well. That might help. Maybe. But you couldn't tell who was driving a car from above.

Then, when he was ten minutes away from his place, the radio crackled. "Cadell? You read?"

"I read."

"There's a truck parked beside your house. An old red pickup. Anyone you know?"

"Damn it, no!" He floored the vehicle even more, hardly hearing the call for units to head toward his ranch.

LYING ON THE ground curled up with her arms over her head, Dory awaited the blow that might kill her. Except that things weren't going according to George's plan. The ostriches were growing increasingly frantic, but they didn't seem to regard the small ball of human at their feet as a threat. Or anything they even wanted to step on. When she dared to open her eyes, she saw those ostrich feet racing around, coming close, but never striking her.

She heard George cussing, heard the awful sound and smelled the terrible smell of singed feathers every time he prodded one of those poor ostriches. She just wished she had a gun so she could put an end to this. So she could save those birds from more terror and pain.

But she didn't have a weapon and didn't dare move.

Then, wonder of wonders, she heard helicopter rotors overhead. She desperately wanted to look but didn't chance it. She heard George start cussing even more viciously, though. Soon the rotors passed on into the distance.

The cops? Had the cops already discovered she was missing?

Oh, God, please let help come soon. Those birds couldn't take much more, and she hated feeling so helpless to put a stop to George's hatefulness.

George spoke, his voice tight with fury. "I'll get you later, *sis.*"

Then the truck engine started. Risking a kick, she lifted her head a little and saw George taking off. It must have been the cops.

She waited, hoping the birds would settle soon. As they began to quiet, she eased herself into a sitting position and looked at them. Each was pecking at its own feathers, as if to remove the singed ones. And neither of them showed the least interest in her.

CADELL WHEELED INTO his driveway, nearly losing his traction on the gravel and headed straight up it. One lane, a ditch to either side, invisible beneath the cut grasses. No place for anyone to go.

Then he saw the red truck bearing down on him. It, too, appeared to be moving at top speed. Cadell gripped the wheel tighter, his mind made up. He was not going into the ditch. Either that so-and-so would swerve or they were going to meet head-on. He had not the least difficulty imagining who would get the worst of a head-on, and it wasn't going to be his official vehicle with the heavy-duty front bumper, strengthened frame and roll bar.

He had one moment when hesitation pierced him. One moment when terror rose as he realized that Dory could be in that truck. But as it came closer, he could see only one head.

His heart and chest tightened. She might already be dead. Well, if so, she was about to get some company, because for the first time in his life Cadell wanted to commit murder. It was an ugly feeling; he hated it even as it rose in him. But he didn't let go of it.

George had already hurt Dory in ways she'd never recover from. If he'd killed her... Well, he was going to join her. He wasn't fit to share the air with another living soul.

GEORGE CAME CHARGING ON, sure the cop would swerve. But he didn't. There was no place to go except to drive around him. It was mowed flat on either side of the road, dry grasses waving. At the last second, he wrenched the wheel, expecting to bypass the oncoming vehicle.

Except those evenly mowed grasses concealed a ditch.

He jolted to a stop so hard his face hit the steering wheel. Searing pain erupted in his chest, but he ignored it. He pushed the door of the truck open and slid out, scrambling up the ditch and heading for the distant trees. He'd always been a fast runner. He could outrun some cop who lived on doughnuts and coffee.

"Police dog," shouted a male voice. "Stop or he'll bite you."

He kept running, ignoring the command, then he heard a word that made no sense.

"Foos!"

He didn't dare look back. He fixed his gaze on those trees and kept pumping his legs and arms, ignoring the pain in his chest.

CADELL WATCHED DASHER take off after the guy. Off lead, as fast as he could run. Cadell paused to look into the red truck. No Dory.

He stared toward the dog chasing the man and knew he had to go after them. The guy might shoot the dog. His partner. Some things a cop couldn't do.

But he called the news in as he began to run and was assured cops were converging at his place, with a chopper standing by if needed. They'd find Dory. He had to finish his job.

The sirens blared behind him. Then, to his great pleasure, other K-9s on the hunt fell into line behind Dasher. That meant not far behind them came their handlers.

George didn't stand a chance.

BACK AT THE RANCH, however, perplexity had set in. Several deputies stood around the ostrich pen, and they might as well have scratched their heads.

"I'm fine," Dory said, now sitting upright, legs tucked. "They didn't hurt me. But they're scared because that guy kept poking them with an electric prod. Just back away. Cadell will know what to do when he gets here."

"It might be a while, ma'am," answered one. "He was last seen running with his K-9 after the guy who abandoned the red truck."

For the first time since early morning, Dory felt like smiling. "He is, is he? I hope Dasher shreds my brother. What about my dog, Flash? He got shocked, too."

"The one that was found in town?"

"Probably."

At that the deputy smiled. "He's fine. The vet's going to look him over, but other than refusing to leave your house, he's okay."

Dory breathed a huge sigh of relief, then felt a

warmth in her heart. For Flash. For Cadell. Imagine the dog not wanting to leave her house. "Couldn't coax him away?"

"Not from what I heard. He snapped at anyone who tried."

"He's had a tough morning."

"Seems like he's not the only one," the deputy answered.

No, she thought, letting her head fall back against the ground. No, indeed. All she knew was Cadell had better come back here safe and sound, or she was going to do something she might regret for the rest of her life.

GEORGE DIDN'T GET far into the woods. Dasher bit him on the forearm and hung on, even after George collapsed. Cadell caught up to find his dog holding George's arm like a stuffed toy, which he wouldn't release until Cadell told him to. Cadell pulled his service pistol, took a bead on George and told Dasher to release him. Not that George had much fight left in him. He was having trouble breathing, panting hard.

So instead of the pleasure of putting him in handcuffs, Cadell had to settle for allowing medevac to take him to the hospital. "Cuff him to the gurney," he told the medics. They promised, accepting a set of flex cuffs from him.

Then he and Dasher headed the rest of the way up his private road and found an almost fantastical scene. Under other circumstances he might have laughed.

But there was only one thing he wanted to know. He trotted up to the pen. "Dory? Are you okay?"

She smiled up at him from where she sat inside the ostrich pen. "I'm fine, but my new friends are going to need to see the doc. I don't know how many times George shocked them."

Then, to his utter amazement, one of those ornery birds craned its neck downward and nuzzled Dory gently.

Well, at least one of them had good taste.

"So," she asked, "do you think you can get me out of here?"

HE GOT HER out of the pen with surprisingly little trouble. The birds settled down in their hiding positions, which made him worry. Usually they seemed to take great delight in regarding him balefully from above. He hoped George hadn't hurt them beyond repair.

Though Dory claimed she was quite all right, the paramedics insisted on examining her for shock. When she seemed okay, they warned Cadell to keep an eye on her.

"It could hit at any time," Jess McGregor said. "If it does, bring her in to the clinic or the ER." Then he limped on his artificial leg around to the front of the truck.

Dory didn't want to leave until Mike Windwalker arrived to check the ostriches. Cadell didn't argue with her, although the thing he most wanted to do was get her home and check her out from head to foot. He couldn't believe she had come through this unscathed.

But for the moment all she wanted to talk about was the ostriches, how they'd avoided hurting her even when George was torturing them. She took clear delight in the fact that Dasher had locked onto George's arm and that her brother had been taken cuffed to the hospital. "I hope he has more than a bite," she said.

Cadell almost smiled. "I'm sure he has more. He crashed his truck in the ditch, and when I got to him he was having trouble breathing. I'm betting broken ribs."

"Good. I hear those hurt."

"Like hell," he agreed.

He watched her with appreciation and amazement. The woman he'd first met had seemed pinched, locked inside herself, stalked by fear. Gradually she'd been emerging from her inner prison, at least with him, but right now she seemed to have busted the doors wide-open. The closest she'd ever come to this much happy animation had been in bed with him. Now she was showering the world with it.

He hoped, for her sake, it lasted. It could begin a whole new chapter in her life.

As he drove her home finally, she grew a bit quieter. He could sense her eagerness to see Flash. Mike Windwalker had said he had a bit of singed fur but no burns. She was still on edge about it, though, which he could understand.

But he was growing increasingly edgy himself. This morning, as he'd raced heedlessly over dangerous roads at unsafe speeds, he'd realized he wanted Dory Lake in his life from now on.

All the flags he'd planted after Brenda—warning flags telling him to avoid long-term relationships with women—had become meaningless. Just like that. Unfortunately, you could waste years trying to avoid getting kicked in the gut until you awoke one morning and found yourself utterly vulnerable.

So he was about to get gut punched again. Because now that George would be going to prison for a good long time again, she could pick up the threads of her old life, and he couldn't imagine why in the world she might want to stay here.

If she was emerging from her private hermitage, surely she'd want to test her wings, taste the world she'd been avoiding. Hell, she hadn't even really dated, from what he could tell. Wouldn't she want to do some sampling? Look for a life in a city with more action? Dang, she'd been in prison as long as her brother had.

And she'd only come here because she thought she could hide and she knew Betty. She'd be crazy not to look for something better.

The signs were all around anyway. She'd set up her office, but she was still using a rickety dining table in her kitchen. She hadn't prettied up even a single corner of the place by hanging a picture. Leaving almost no mark that she had been there.

So, she was planning to move on quickly. Nothing was permanent, not even the high-speed internet she'd had installed, and that was a cord that could be severed with a phone call.

Of course, he had only himself to blame. The flags had been there from the beginning. He should have known better than to break his own rule. Women couldn't be trusted to stay. Brenda had proved that.

When they got to her house, Flash was still on the porch waiting. Someone had put a bowl of water out for him, but he was concerned about only one thing.

When Dory climbed out of the SUV, Flash dashed toward her, forgot all his training and jumped up on her, knocking her to the patchy front lawn.

Cadell listened to her giggle as Flash licked her face, and he smiled faintly, poised to leave. She didn't need him anymore.

But then she freed herself from Flash's attentions and jumped to her feet. "Come on in," she said to Cadell. "I don't know about you, but I could really use some coffee."

He hesitated. "I was just about to go."

She froze. "Why?"

"You must have stuff you want to do."

"Stuff?" She tilted her head. "Okay, then. You're on my list of stuff. Come inside."

He took his usual place at the rickety kitchen table while she fed Flash, then started the coffee.

Then she faced him. "So tell me something, Deputy Marcus. Was I just a job to you?"

He felt almost sickened by the question. "What?" He didn't want to believe she'd just said that.

"All the nights you spent here. Was that just protection, like Flash? You said you were a protector. Was that all I was? A job?"

Her words punched him. "No," he said hoarsely.

"Then why are you in such a hurry to leave?"

His self-control was usually pretty good, but after the stressors of that day, it had frayed. The words burst from him, almost angrily. "Because you're getting ready to leave now that George is no longer a threat."

She frowned. "Did I say that? I don't remember ever saying that."

"Well, why the hell would you want to stay here?"

Her face changed, and he thought he detected a flicker of the fear that had once been there so often. When she spoke, her voice was small. "You?"

Astonishment gripped him. Before he could respond, she'd turned her back to him, reaching for mugs.

"I realize," she said, "that you don't want another woman in your life. I get it. Brenda must have been the witch of all witches. Anyway, maybe you're done with me. Maybe I was just a job to you. Regardless, I'm not leaving. I don't want to leave. I want joint custody."

Now he was confused. "Joint custody of what?"

"Itsy and Bitsy."

That did it. Circuitous as she was being, he got it. Being willfully dense would serve nothing. He shoved the chair back so hard it tipped over.

She whirled, startled by the sound, and he was amazed to see tears rolling down her cheeks.

"Those ostriches," he said firmly, "don't come without *me*."

She wiped the tears away with her sleeve, but her smile still hadn't appeared. "You'd better mean that."

"I never meant anything more in my life. We're a package, me and those birds. Take it or leave it."

The smile began to peek out. "I'll take it," she said quietly.

He grabbed her then, forgetting finesse, drawing her into a hug so tight she squeaked. "You take it, you can't leave it."

"I couldn't possibly leave those birds," she said shakily.

He closed his eyes, pressed his lips to her hair and muttered, "So I have to keep them?"

"If you want me."

"I guess I'm stuck with them. Because I love you."

She threw her arms around his neck, and he felt his uniform shirt dampen with her warm tears. "I love you, too, Cadell. I want you, the dogs, the ostriches… I want it all."

"Babies?"

Her head tipped back. "Babies," she agreed firmly. "But you get joint custody."

Finally he laughed. It was the most joyous sound that had escaped him in a long time. "I'll help with it all."

She pressed her lips to his, giving him a salty kiss. "Forever."

"Forever," he repeated. "Forever."

* * * * *

If you loved this suspenseful story by
New York Times *bestselling author Rachel Lee,*
don't miss out on previous books in the
CONARD COUNTY:
THE NEXT GENERATION
miniseries:

UNDERCOVER IN CONARD COUNTY
CONARD COUNTY MARINE
CONARD COUNTY SPY
A SECRET IN CONARD COUNTY

Available now from Harlequin Romantic Suspense!